KU-471-612

Bedside
SKIING

John Samuel

Bedside
SKIING

Illustrations by S. McMurtry

Stanley Paul
London Melbourne Sydney Auckland Johannesburg

Stanley Paul & Co. Ltd

An imprint of Century Hutchinson Ltd
62-65 Chandos Place, London WC2N 4NW
Century Hutchinson (Australia) Pty Ltd
16-22 Church Street, Hawthorn, Melbourne, Victoria 3122
Century Hutchinson (NZ) Ltd
191 Archers Road, Glenfield, Auckland 10
Century Hutchinson (SA) Pty Ltd
PO Box 337, Bergvlei 2012, South Africa

First published 1987
Copyright © in text John Samuel 1987
Copyright © in illustrations Lennard Books 1987

Made by Lennard Books Ltd
Mackerye End, Harpenden, Herts AL5 5DR

Editor Michael Leitch
Designed by Pocknell & Co

British Library Cataloguing in Publication Data
Samuel, John
    Bedside Skiing.
    I. Title
828'.91407   PN6175

ISBN 0 09 171430 3

Printed and bound in Great Britain by
Butler & Tanner Ltd,
Frome, Somerset.

CONTENTS

PREFACE

This is a collection of personal, fun experiences in 30 years of skiing and ski writing, most of it for *The Guardian*. It has never been a full-time occupation. While in the Fifties and Sixties skiing was a sport ripe for expansion, and one legitimately to be pursued for an expanding national newspaper, it was also an escape to places where the sports editor's phone did not endlessly ring.

It has meant a lot of laughs and many friends worldwide. I am especially grateful to Nick Howe for snowy reminders of New Hampshire's colonial past; Erna Low, for her one-woman Austrian colonization of Britain; and Jimmy Riddell for his memories of first love on Swiss snow and ice.

Also to my daughter, Carah, enough of a chip to spend a repping winter grilling on one of Courchevel's lower levels.

Finally to my wife, Mary, who has never reached the top of any ski tow in any kind of order, and who lets me go, ski bag and baggage, with the least envious of waves.

INTRODUCTION

I have the sort of mind that begins at the beginning and ends heaven knows where. Early impressions are strong and I can remember exactly how I became a left-handed batsman at cricket. I was four years old and the bat an older boy gave me was half my size. 'What are you going to be, left-handed or right?' I was asked by my eight-year-old mentor.

'I don't know,' I wailed, 'I can't hold it either way.'

'Then be a left-hander. You'll be more awkward for the bowlers.' I am left-handed in nothing else, not even golf. As a right-hander I might have played for England . . .

I come from Sussex and cricket was part of my Wealden heritage. Skiing was different. You needed to be two-footed and two-handed. Also, you couldn't do it in Sussex; so it was that another friend, a rather truer one, first suggested going to Norway, in 1954. It had a noble, wild prospect; mysterious fjords where giant battleships had lurked. I live today in an old coach house whose grounds briefly harboured the first British paratroops to drop in anger; and then they went to Norway. In the great passage of arms and people that had been part of my childhood, Norway stood out. I remembered, wonderingly, how German paratroopers had been dropped without their 'chutes straight into snow drifts, and nearly all had survived.

Snow already had a fascination, but it was inextricably linked with the local ice rink, the SS Brighton. Far from being a beached paddle-steamer, this was where Alan Weeks earned his broadcaster stripes in the heady atmosphere of Brighton Tigers versus Harringay Racers or Nottingham Panthers. On Saturday and Sunday mornings our Jayne Torvills, transformed out of their gym-slips, magically performed leggy pirouettes and even double-axels. It was where we learned that falling over was fun, and not just when it was someone else.

Norway, then, seemed a great idea. We were, I suppose, Bronze Age skiers. No plastic slopes with uniformed BASI instructors. Only two tour operators that I knew about went to the snow – Erna Low and Inghams. My friend, who had already dug out Neville Cardus's autobiography for our self-improvement, also discovered a course run by the Central Council of Physical Recreation. For about £50 we could learn to ski at Geilo. The Bergen-Oslo line, an overnight boat journey out of Newcastle, represented an exhilarating touch of freedom.

In 1903 Sir Arnold Lunn, subsequently founder of the Kandahar Racing Club and inventor of the slalom ski race, discovered that equipment to some extent dictated his skiing ability. 'On my first pair of skis,' he recounted, 'I could not turn abruptly without my foot coming right off the ski. I reduced speed by leaning heavily on a single pole. I zig-zagged across steeper slopes and kick-turned to change direction. On the gentler slopes I stopped by dragging myself round my single pole. I skied for three winters before I saw a skier execute S-turns down a slope.'

I was shortly to find something similar. Skiing is a sport where performance is inevitably linked to equipment and attitude. My first purchase was a pair of ski boots in a closing-down sale. Early seeds of failure were in those boots. Even in Norway, not notably a radical country, they were politely set down as antiques. They were leather, but, and it was a big but, they were essentially climbing boots. The leather gave out at the ankle bone, just enough to bruise, not enough to support. As instruments of foot torture they were unparalleled.

In Geilo we lined up in khaki unisex hand-me-downs. Early January in Norway means a sun lolling along the southern horizon like a melon too long on the stall. Selection was distinctly sexist. Lively looking young men in one group, the girls and the pudgier men in the other. Stig, who had paddled across the North Sea single-handed to join the RAF, was our instructor.

He was now an Oslo barrister who instructed for pleasure, or so we were told. The threat he held over the men for ten days was that we would be banished to join the women if we did not come up to scratch. We were 1950s men, not long out of national service, from single-sex schools where to be dropped from the first team was a fate little short of death. It was a potent threat.

Our skis were wooden, 200 centimetres long, with variable Kandahar bindings. The wire of the binding could be reset on the lugs of the ski so that we could lift our heels two to three inches for touring skiing. The wire needed to be tightened, clamping our heels firmly to the skis, for downhill skiing.

ANTIQUES

PONG

Stig taught us the plough turn. This is the inverted V position, tips of the skis close together but not quite touching, tails splayed out behind, by which the skier first gets down the hill under some sort of control. Today, with infinitely more sophisticated equipment, you still see children up to about 14 quite naturally and capably getting down the mountain using the same basic V. If you put more weight on the right ski you will turn left, and if more on the left you will turn right. As all skiers above the absolute beginners know, it is like learning to row – with the boat turning the opposite way to the one you at first expect.

Stig's benevolent tyranny for me represented a plough turn cast in concrete in the memory. It was another ten years before the last vestiges of his teaching, plus plastic boots and infinitely more sophisticated skis and bindings, eliminated the instinctive reaction to plough, especially in poor light or bad snow. Early learning requires a flexibility. It helps if you understand why the simple-looking object a ski appears to be is shaped exactly as it is. The ski is about as simple as a beautiful woman. The mountain is as dependable as a handsome man. Their marriage . . . well, watch out for the bumps.

REPORTER ON TOUR

Some years ago I presented some bills to the taxman for a padded suit and a pair of skis. The Inland Revenue inquired loftily, 'Do you need to ski to write about skiing?' By that, I am sure, they meant race skiing.

Well, I suppose not, if you only stand at the end of a downhill run, bribe your way into David Vine's commentary box, or squint at the press TV monitor over the shoulder of a hefty Austrian. You could save a lot of time and expense by sitting at home and watching Saturday's *Grandstand* programme with a glass of light ale in your hand. One report, though, would easily read like another, and sooner or later your readers would rumble you. Moreover, as most of us know, the camera eye does not see all. Nor, with only two minutes between top runners, and a minute and a half between the rest, does the commentator – any commentator.

Ski racing makes an outstanding test for a greenhorn reporter. An Outward Bound course can help, to begin with. Then SAS Territorial Army training on storming a Jäger Division stronghold. Four weeks of Berlitz German and French can see you all but ready for the fray. A short refresher course on iced-up cameras, tape recorders and hand brakes may help; so will a few rounds with the light gloves to get you in shape for Geneva's Baggage Reclaim.

Preparations presume a minimum of 12 weeks on the artificial slopes of Sandown Park, Telford, Hillend or suchlike. Nothing like a bit of nyl-brush to beat a bit of discipline into you.

What to pack can snare the unwary. Old troopers know that ski firms may be hurling demo skis at them the moment they set foot in Bormio or Crans. These may be worth buying in for the kids, perhaps, but better the devil you know for what lies ahead, so you take your known and trusted skis and boots.

Thus the first law of travel –
two items of luggage only, one for each hand – is
flouted. You've three items: main bag containing office
(word processor, reference files and books), boot bag, ski bag.
Any one of the British Airways Authority's prime sites, Gatwick,
Heathrow and Manchester, will provide the first modular test: how
to load your skis on the standard luggage cart. Answer – you don't. Tips or
tails simply won't lodge. You sling the bag over your shoulder and push on
regardless. Even the expert may need reminding that carts don't go up and down
escalators as they do in Zürich and Geneva. Forgetfulness on this score can prove
embarrassing if not necessarily fatal.

Disembarkation is no less fraught. Even the orderly Swiss are still wedded to
the notion that Mr Average Briton will ski on bananas if these are what he is offered
at the resort hire shop. Baggage Reclaim is often overwhelmed by the Salomon,
Atomic and Snow and Rock bags bursting out of the BAC-III charter holds. Mostly,
of course, your skis get through. When they don't, be patient with the young ladies
comparing love lives at the Lost Luggage desk. Franz and Jules give them a tough
time. If you've gone out by British Air Tours don't forget later to check with Dan
Air, Cathay Pacific, American Airlines . . . or vice versa. Luggage tracing is not an
exact science.

Hopefully, our tyro ski writer will survive unscathed.

Getting there in one piece is part of the fun. Geneva airport, one of the important gateways to France's Winter Olympic stations, is artfully constructed to defeat the Anglo-Saxon sense of logic. One area is in Switzerland, the other in France. Such signs as exist are intended to dupe. It is clear that the Swiss and the French don't exactly get on. The French would have preferred you came via Lyons anyway.

Young ladies who've got up at 4 am cover themselves with welcoming smiles and present tour operator notices. One by one and bit by bit they round up the milling punters. In the coaches they play the numbers game. At the fifth count they will be a couple short. Somewhere in the Arrive or Depart buildings will be those desperately seeking a loo sign, peering at the French sector rather than the Swiss – a classic error.

Our tyro ski writer may well find himself Thomsonated or Inghamized before he has separated Switzerland from France. He should be so lucky. The roads to the Tarantaise are best left to the professional coach drivers. If he can smuggle himself aboard a tour operator coach, so much the better.

Do-it-yourself means a hire car. Inevitably it is not the car you ordered. Sometimes they upgrade you, which means the very rear-wheel-drive saloon you tried so hard to avoid. It is not skierized as you had so hopefully demanded. It has regular tyres for the diplomat or businessman who will never leave Geneva. Or Zürich. Or Munich. Your request for winter tyres is received with bewilderment. Only the British could make such a fuss. Roof rack? You are suddenly aware what it is like to ask for rat poison in a pharmacist.

Ah yes, a front-wheel drive. But why winter tyres on the front and not on the back? They give you a strange look. 'Everyone puts regular tyres on the back . . . In any case, there's no snow.' Too true. There often isn't. Weather patterns are changing all over the world. We're a degree warmer than in the Twenties and Thirties. The snow comes later. It's to do with ozone layers and aerosols, traffic emission too. We with our hire cars must bear our share of guilt. It's winter tyres on the front and like it. So off we squirm to our World Cup destinations.

ROMANCE AND THE SKI

Skis have a romantic history. I have fallen in love with a particular pair many times. Never out of love. Before they become old, floppy-flexed and rusty-edged, I try to find them a good home with novice skiers who will briefly cherish them before moving on to better things.

Skis, so pure and apparently simple in appearance, are complex precision instruments – like an unspoiled country girl, someone once said. Billy Johnson, the US Olympic champion, was asked if he kept his favourite skis under his bed. 'No,' he answered. 'In it.' I have never challenged his priorities.

Men have become infatuated with the design of skis, or their belief in certain materials. To them the ski is a kind of mistress. It's hard to believe anyone felt that way about the oldest known ski, the 2,500-year-old Ovrebo in the ski museum of the Holmenkollen, Oslo. It is a simple board. But there is no accounting for tastes.

The solid hickory mountain touring ski of the 1920s was succeeded in the Thirties by the Splitkein, with thin layers of different woods glued together on the plywood principle for a much stronger and more resilient article. You could layer it like a sandwich or a neapolitan ice cream. The standard issue for the US Army's Tenth Mountain Division was designed to repel all boarders. Nick Hock, publisher of *Skiing* magazine, recalls, 'You could ski for two weeks in powder snow without once seeing your skis. They were like submarines.'

Harry and Hart Holmberg introduced the first metal ski, called the Hart, in 1955. Howard Head, a Martin aircraft engineer who could not ski, when asked to design a pair for someone who could, came up with the I-beam principle with top and bottom skins connected by a core. The Head Standard that emerged became the breakthrough ski of the Fifties, the famous Cheater that changed the nature of ski construction for all time. It had an aluminium top and bottom, plastic sides, and a core of sandwich plywood layers set on edge. It was a typically American production job which by design quality and price brought skiing within reach of a mass public. It turned with wonderful ease, it did not warp, it needed no special care. Its one great drawback made it a failure as a racing ski. Metal vibrates rapidly and it jumped about too much at speed. Head introduced rubber as a damper, but resisted glass fibre. The only time he tried it the skis turned pink, presumably with embarrassment.

Franz Kneissl, Austrian heir to a coach and wheel factory close by the Bavarian border at Kufstein, jumped in with a fibreglass casing from which emerged the legendary White Star. Man and machine came together with the young racer Karl Schranz. On the other side of the Alps, the French firm of Dynamic were employing glass fibre in sheets. Wrapped round the core, mummy-like, it gave the soft tip and firm tail enabling a racer named Jean-Claude Killy to exploit new French techniques pioneered by two ski 'professors', Georges Joubert and Jean Vuarnet. With the skier leaning forward, the ski would carve a strict route through the snow with no time-wasting skid. Out of corners he could seemingly sit back more. The appearance of this was often misleading. All top skiers stay very central over their skis. But the jet forward obtained from the stiffer tails could never be gainsaid. The ski world tossed around the newest catchword for the technique – *avalement*. This was the Sixties. Availment was the name of the game.

The gaunt and soulful Killy was the skier of the era with his three gold medals at the 1968 Grenoble Winter Olympic Games. Winner, too, of the first World Cup series in 1967 and again in 1968.

The Seventies brought in its Clint Eastwood – the Austrian Karl Schranz. No love was lost between Schranz and the tough old Chicago millionaire Avery Brundage, president of the International Olympic Committee. Schranz, in a throwaway interview with the veteran Associated Press sports editor, Will Grimsley, ventured to suggest that people who accepted money for skiing (shhh, pros) would one day ski in the Olympics. No-one truly foresaw the consequences. Brundage expelled him from the 1972 Sapporo Games in what he thought was disgrace. Schranz went home to an idolizing Viennese crowd of a quarter of a million, and to the beginning of the end of old-style amateurism.

Just as Schranz upheld Kneissl for many years, Annemarie Moser-Proell, the fag-smoking Austrian tigress of the 1970s, did as much for the small-town ski-

maker, Alois Rohrmoser. When he spotted the 13-year-old Wunderkind on
wooden skis and ancient cable bindings, Rohrmoser was making 32,000 Atomic
skis a year. It was 700,000 by the time Annemarie came through with six World
Cup titles and, finally in 1980, Olympic gold. Annemarie invested in the Café
Annemarie in her home village of Kleinarl, married one of Rohrmoser's
representatives, Herbert Moser, and set the six crystal globes awarded for World
Cup titles in a showcase. Love was once again conquering all. While she was
zooming down ski slopes at 70 mph, Herbert sold World Cup T-shirts and
Annemarie's autographed postcards with the Vienna coffee and the apfel strudel.

Annemarie's flat features, pale blue eyes and hair saved from mousiness by a
tinge of Celtic red, were no more conventionally glamorous than her coiled hawser
figure. Her immediate celebration after a win was a puff on a tipped cigarette. But,
when she retired just before the 1976 Innsbruck Winter Olympic Games, Austria
reeled. Rohrmoser, it was said, was being too stingy. More to the point, she was
nursing her dying father and herself undergoing a stomach operation.

As the bills slowly mounted she took the decision to race again. First, though,
she had to satisfy the Olympic authorities she was totally suitable, even for these
enlightened days. Heavens! It came to light that she had made $7,750 from a
television commercial showing her triumphing, not over a death-defying downhill
course, but a horrid-looking jelly stain. After pained negotiations she made over
the fee to the Austrian Ski Federation. In 1980, at the age of 26, she won her first
Olympic gold medal at Lake Placid, bombing down the mountain in a whiter than
white suit as no other woman has achieved before or since. And Herbert was able
to tell the world, 'Now she stay at home and get children.'

A TO Z OF SKI

No ski book should be without an A to Z. Usually, though, it comes at the end, which is all wrong. My glossary will gloss over nothing, and is essential early reading.

A

Abfahrt (Ger) Indispensable if you want to get to know the German language. In ski it means a downhill race. At the railway station or airport it means departure or starting time. Either way it reduces the English to helpless giggles. Other **-fahrt** words are *Ausfahrt* outway or excursion; *Einfahrt* in way or entrance; and *Fahrt* quite simply, way.

Abonnement (Fr) A season ticket for lifts, more usually for a week, sometimes divided into A, B or C packages. Inevitably, on the coach up from Geneva, Bill or Tom has sussed it out better, so you make the rep's job hell by switching your ordered A to B (or C), demanding money back in francs. The lift lady, meanwhile, has not received her tour operator's cheque, so Day One turns out a right stew for all concerned.

Artificial slope Ski area where Britons never never will be slaves. No other nationality deems them salutory or necessary. A fall on a bristle slope, we apparently believe, turns boys into men.

Avalement (Fr) Technique of quick, supple movements, involving fast turns and foot thrusts, perfected by British chalet girls on return to the Saturday night guest binge after an evening with Hans or Jules. Also: *Non-avalement* This is when you don't make it.

B

Bahnhof (Ger) Bar outside which some people get on and off trains. Cheapest booze in the place, usually occupied by English upper classes wearing squeaky voices and funny wool bonnets; especially at St Anton.

Ballet Part of freestyle, a demo event at the Calgary Olympics, where TV moguls expect the girls to show off their knickers, but get it confused with aerials, bumps and triple salchows.

Base lodge Peculiarly American way of getting together at the bottom of a mountain.

BASI British Association of Ski Instructors. SAS group trained to occupy mountain redoubts of Andorra, Cairngorms, Glencoe and Glenshee, and bristling fortifications of Hillend, Bearsden, Telford, Sandown Park, etc. A crack foreign legion exciting envy and hatred (especially among the French).

Basket Disc near base of ski pole limiting penetration of the snow. To the British, any foreigner.

Biathlon Skiing and shooting. As the *cognoscenti* know, the British have a better record at this than any winter sport barring poncy twisting and turning on skates. Has yet to be discovered and adapted by Union Jack-bearing supporters.

Bindings Behaviour patterns encouraging the ski rep to mix bromide or poison to the **Glühwein**. As in 'My room overlooks the dustbins not the mountains.' Or 'I am a parallel skier, please move me up a class tomorrow.' Also: attachment of boot to ski.

Birdsnesting The art of arranging one duvet round two persons. Also: finding new ways in quiet necks of the woods.

Black run Difficult, steep run, stumbled upon by near-parallel skiers who've left the route map in their bedroom; described in tedious detail over the chalet teapot.

Bloodwagon Stretcher on runners usually parked somewhere near the warmest mid-mountain restaurant, usually, to everyone's disappointment, empty of humanity.

Blue run No bumps, not too steep, no ice, packed snow, what many people love to scorn in the evening having skied it most of the day.

Brake What some old-timers tried to do with a single pole stuck between the legs. More recently, a spring-loaded prong attached to the binding to stop a ski from sliding after a fall.

Bubble Key element of essential US ski artefact, the jacuzzi. Also: gondola-style lift.

Bum-bag Belted receptacle positioned above posterior. Should not be unzipped *in situ* but swung round above navel to delve in without risk of loss.

C

Cable-car Large moving cabin suspended from overhead line. Beloved of thriller writers, for obvious reasons.

Camber Tilt in icy road, especially dangerous for après-skiers. Also: arched shape of ski, not discernible to the naked eye after three months of non-stop deployment at the hire shop.

Carved turn Precise, high-speed turn impossible to accomplish on any ski which won't reverse **camber** into the snow when weighted.

Chair lift Easy riding in Colorado sunshine, latitude of Sicily. In northern Alps, term used to describe refrigerated occasional transport.

Chalet Austrian or Swiss house with steep gables, acquired in large numbers by the British in the name of Empire, offering a tea-time cuppa and never having to speak to the natives or pay their exorbitant prices.

Chill factor The cool, fresh wind in the hair which sends body temperature diving (see also **chair lift**).

Christiania Old name for Oslo, where they invented turns on wood skis still favoured by Surrey Alp veterans.

Circus Lifts linking a set of runs on different mountains round the base camp zoo.

Compact ski Short ski, easy to manoeuvre, ideal beginner tool, thus heavily discouraged in case people get too good too soon and won't go to ski school any more.

Cross-country World's No 1 aerobic exercise. Goes with nuts, fruit and vegetables. Not so popular in villages making pots of money in *Weinstube, Konditorei, Bierkeller, Pferdestall* or wherever *Gemütlichkeit* is marketed. In other languages you get *Langlauf* (Ger); *Ski de fond* (Fr); *Langrenn* (Scand); *XC* (Am).

D

DIN German measuring standard for ski equipment and noise levels. Readily adapted by Anglo-Saxons (i.e. British and Americans) from their distant cousins.

Downhill Measuring standard for last season's form as opposed to this. Also: ski race for the brave and/or foolhardy.

Drag lift Means of getting reluctant novice uphill.

E

Edging Queue-jumping device, using outside flanks.
Eingang (Ger) German equivalent to British Benidorm brigade. Also: entrance.

F

Fall-line Easiest place to fall, i.e. most direct line down the mountain.
Fasching (Ger) Boisterous Lenten carnival with prices to match.
Fermé (Fr) Thus far and no farther. Precipice, dynamiters, etc., ahead! Also: *Geschlossen, Gesperrt* (both Ger).
Föhn (Ger) Warm wind producing thaw, suicides. Also: *Chinook* (Canadian).
Funicular Ancient tracked railway on steep slopes. Beloved of Swiss and Italian tenors.

G

Gasthaus (Ger) Small Austrian boarding house where old ladies exercise German on guests, gassing about family origins and fecundity.
Glühwein (Ger) Hot, spicy wine, stimulant to end-of-day bragging. Also: *vin chaud* (Fr).

H

Herringbone Choking way of climbing uphill.

J

Joch Kilted skier. Also: pass linking two peaks.
Jump turn 'Expert' way of lifting ski tails out of heavy or crusty snow. Often involuntary.

K

Kandahar Codename for British ski invasion of Alps in 1924, setting up HQ in Mürren, Switzerland. Operations include invention of slalom and downhill aided by less hostile natives such as Swiss Academic Ski Club. Derives from Lord Roberts of Kandahar, Afghanistan, who never skied but was persuaded to present a trophy. Operation **K~** involved successful storming of St Anton (Austria), Garmisch-Partenkirchen (West Germany) and Chamonix (France). First C-in-C, Arnold Lunn, succeeded by James Bond, who overthrew wicked Blofeld in 1969. Codenames of successful operations include Inferno, Risorgimento, Scaramanga Roped. Also: name of first World Ski Championships, held at **K~** Club, Mürren 1931.

Kick turn 'Easy' way of changing direction by 180 degrees when faced by precipice or other impassable hazard. Often paralytically difficult.

L

Lehrer (Ger) German-speaking ski instructor, sometimes pronounced 'liar' or 'leerer'. Note: no Austrian learns from an instructor, he knows it already. **L~**, like Fr *moniteurs*, exist to teach skiing to the British, Dutch, German carriage trade in 6/12 days. Qualifications: (1) ability to lead others down a mountain trail a touch above class standard, thus proving necessity of ski school. (2) ability to make themselves pleasant with simple jokes, winks and smiles, and ready knowledge of best feet-up spots on mountain.

Loipe (Nor) Marked cross-country trail. For the serious get-fitter or queue copper-out. Also: *Loop.*

Low season Ever-diminishing periods of regular as opposed to high pricing, e.g. snowless weeks before Christmas; the two weeks or so between New Year and Fasching; a few days between traditional February school hols and Easter.

M

Moguls Dynasty of bumpy slopes invented in US by default, i.e. left ungroomed by omnipresent snow tractors.

Motorway Broad, easy, well-groomed **piste**, universally despised and universally used.

N

Nursery slope Gentle beginner area. Often, brownish tracts close to older villages, their disused lifts a museum item for non-skiers or ski historians.

O

Offen (Ger) Run open, but may be worn or icy. First run always requires care. Also: *Ouvert* (Fr).

Off-piste Unpatrolled, unmarked areas of natural snow. Beloved of powder hounds whose risk-taking can end tragically with the avalanche sniffer dogs, but more likely offer the second best experience available to man or womankind. Where good guides are truly worth their salt.

Outside ski In a traverse or turn, the ski on the downhill side. Conversely, inside ski equals uphill ski. Also: what novice skiers often feel after ski instruction – turned inside out.

P

Piste (Fr) Marked, prepared run, sometimes with bumps (moguls) caused by repeated passage of skiers down steeper sections. Also: *On the piste . . . Piste off* – clichés the regular skier must seek to survive.

Pole Pointed stick with grip, useful for opening bindings, admonishing queue-jumpers, drawing maps in the snow, holding far in front of the body in best potty-trained style, flipping flippantly for going round corners.

Poma Not an endangered mountain species, but a form of lift needing care and experience on mounting, etc. A plate is passed between the legs for the buttocks to take the strain as the line tautens and hauls the skier up a prepared track of various bumps and hollows.

Porridge Prison sentence meted out to queue-jumpers in the more serious ski countries like Scotland. Also refers to sticky, lumpy snow.

Powder snow New, low-temperature, light-textured snow bringing bays of delight from experts, and a sick feeling in the stomach for the unaggressive intermediate who's not sure how to handle it.

R

Ratrac Snow tractor providing corrugated, beaten surface leading to sick feeling in the stomach, etc. Also: *Snow cat, Piste basher.*

S

Schuss (Ger) Straight run down the fall-line which everyone practises at once around 4 pm in the average French resort.

Scissors turn The kind of racer turn taught in ski schools which top racers scissored out of their repertoire the season before.

Sideslip Sideways slide down a hill producing the most spectacular of domino accidents when the back-marker tips over onto the rest.

Slalom Race invented by British public schoolboys who stopped short at the lashing hinged-pole beatings of modern Continental practice.

Snowplough Grotesque movement down or near the fall-line, skis in a V position, tips forward.

Steilhang (Ger) Especially steep slope, or ice wall, where sadistic **Lehrer** will lead advanced class to show who's boss.

T

Telemark Turning by a kind of skiing curtsy. Possible only on cross-country skis where the boot is not bound to the ski by the heel.
Tip Helpful information. Includes sort you give your enemies, e.g. Park your skis separately at the mid-mountain restaurant, ensuring you lose one or both. Also refers to point at front of ski, helpful in dealing with queue-jumping foreigners.
Trail American mountain run, usually named with bags of imagination, e.g. Plunge, Moment of Truth, Corkscrew, Adios, Never Ever . . .
Tuck Low crouch, also known as the egg position, adopted by professional downhillers going fast and amateurs who, US egg fashion, may end up 'easy and over'.

W

Wedel (Ger) Set of linked recoveries.
White-out Skiing without seeing. Truth, moment of . . .

Z

Ziel (Ger) Pron. zeal, meaning finish of a race, or the bottom line.

OUR MAN IN THE GIANT SLALOM

Tuesday 9 February 1987, and David Miller of *The Times* reported from the World Alpine Ski Championships at Crans-Montana, Switzerland:

'For the first time in the Championships the Swiss had no medal . . . Zurbriggen fell on the second run, an occurrence receiving only marginally more attention in the Press Centre than the disqualification of the expert from *The Guardian* before reaching even the first gate of the media's giant slalom.'

Now it can be told. I'd had a breakfast interview date with the belle of the Championships, Switzerland's haughtily lovely Maria Walliser, winner of two gold medals, in the beauty salon of the Swiss women's hotel. I was much intrigued that a country so slow with the vote for women should be so quick with the sophisticated needs of make-up and blow-dry for their women athletes. They were the first team ever with a beauty salon to go with the wax room.

Suzy Wolf, a hairdresser and beauty specialist, had found a sponsor, Wella, and talked the Swiss Ski Federation into it. She told me Maria was loaded the night before the women's downhill – loaded with electricity. Who would know that better than a hairdresser?

The chatter was sufficient fun to make me late for the press race. You think you know where it's being held. Always you seem to be poling away to some other part of the mountain. It's not so much a Freudian desire to miss it, it's simply a low-priority occasion and you don't pay enough attention.

Eventually I found myself on the right gondola and as I passed over the start area saw the first few tying on their bibs. It was going to be tight. I was Number 32 and they'd be starting two or three to the minute. The run from the gondola mid-station took in a practice slalom slope – steep and slushy in the warm sunshine. Worse. Soldiers were trying to remove safety netting, which I would have to bypass.

As I got there I realized I didn't have time for that. Sliding towards the nylon snake I made up my mind to jump it. Alas I had no bump to work with. The leap was pretty pathetic, and the tip of a ski neatly hooked the netting. Off came the ski and I went tumbling. Cursing, I put myself together again and pushed off for the start.

I could quickly tell there was trouble. No. 32 was next and he hadn't showed. Then they spotted me. I remember a Japanese photographer friend's anxious face and 'Quick, John, over here.' I checked momentarily at the gate, then vaulted away. In any race you are supposed to leave your mind in the start gate. Mine was still with me, none too pleased at my goings-on.

I got too low in a traverse and half-fell. A second time it was worse. Trying to step up to make the gate I tripped and fell, losing a ski. Clipping it on again seemed to take an age. I was out of sight of the finish. It was all going on in a vacuum.

At the finish no-one seemed to be noticing. They were all knocking back the Liffy Water of our sponsors. 'How did you do?' one of the British racers, Lesley Beck, asked. I began preparing a suitable mumble about my two falls. As I opened my mouth someone yelled, 'You're disqualified. They've just announced it. What did you do?'

In my panic I'd set off too quickly, before the start gate wand was set. If you don't break it you don't set the clock going, even with your best jump start. Disqualification, I decided on the instant, was a better way to go than lamely falling. I shrugged like a man denied an Olympic medal by a petty infraction. 'At least I went for it,' I heard myself saying. 'The only way,' said Lesley. I'm sure my words, if not my example, helped her to tenth place in the slalom.

As for Miller . . . he should have been there.

THE SKI INDUSTRY

Sir Arnold Lunn, who laid down most of the rules of modern ski racing, believed that all sport involved the invention of difficulties for the sheer fun of solving them. He lived long enough to see the Edwardian conception of sport – something that mattered desperately while you were doing it, but not at all when you stopped – completely altered.

Skiing is now an industry. Its top racers are dollar millionaires, their incomes deriving from a huge commercial complex. The average holiday skier, poised to start his run from the top of the mountain, represents a personal investment of around £600 worth of skis, bindings, boots, poles, suit, gloves, hat, goggles, sun cream and, arguably, last but not necessarily least, bum-bag. My eight-year-old daughter was delighted at the chance to say such a naughty word legitimately and couldn't wait to get her hands on one.

Equipment is, however, only part of the story. There is a journey by plane, car or bus to a base village. An hotel or apartment has been booked. There is also something called a duplex which roughly resembles a cross-section of a wardrobe; impoverished youngsters favour these as they are usually cheaper and undoubtedly cosier. Chalet parties are also popular. The hugger-mugger of guests are looked after by a team of Sloaney chalet girls who do English country house teas as well as an evening meal. The atmosphere is hearty and jolly and, at tea time, quite steamy as damp socks dry off on radiators while their owners lick the cream from their fingers and bury their noses in mugs of hot tea.

The support systems don't end at equipment, travel and accommodation. There is usually a travel agent involved at the booking stage and each of the thousands of ski villages in Europe and America employs an army of cooks, cleaners, porters, drivers, couriers, waiters and ski lift attendants, to name but a few of the support jobs. Mountain transportation is extremely expensive and is needed to carry supplies as well as skiers. It probably doesn't often occur to the average skier, relaxing on a sunlit terrace, how the soup and pommes frites he has just enjoyed actually got up there. Here is how.

KEEPING THEM HAPPY

Q. What goes up, and up, and up, and never comes down?

A. The price of mountain food.

Let's be fair to mountain restaurant prices the world over. It doesn't come cheap feeding the 5,000-plus who ski a big mountain.

At Vail, Colorado, four to six bakers work a daily 12-hour shift, mixing and kneading dough, to bake more than 100 dozen loaves, 60 dozen doughnuts, 30 dozen croissants, 30 dozen apple fritters and 10 dozen Danish rolls to keep the folks on the mountain topped up with carbohydrate.

All night, three cooks stir massive cauldrons brewing 360 gallons of soup, 300 gallons of chili con carne, and 200 gallons of stew. In the ovens, 300 lb of ribs, 250 lb of barbecue meat and 40 gallons of baked beans gently sizzle.

Throughout the night, trucks convoy the food and many tons of beer, wine and soft drinks to gondolas for the trip up the mountain. Four prime restaurants serve 10,000 and more skiers on an average day. The cupboard must never be bare. When the skiing ends for the day, another kind of après-ski gets moving. The snow tractor Panzer division start work as soon as the last lifts are closed. Their job is to fill in the ruts and smooth the bumps on beginner and intermediate trails. At the same time the ski patrol – about 30 at a place like Vail in the US – comb the slopes for lost items, people included. Every so often they will stop and call out, just in case… At the bottom an all-clear message will be flashed up the mountain to patrol headquarters.

Snow from the skies these days is a bonus, certainly at most capital-intensive US resorts trying to attract skiers away from Florida beaches. When the Rockies suffered a snow famine in 1976–77, Governor Lamm of Colorado declared his state a disaster area. In came man-made snow, water and compressed air separately piped up the mountain and fused into 'snow' at sub-zero temperatures through jet-like nozzles.

For much of the night, the snow guns of Aspen and Vail, Stowe and Killington will be bombarding the slopes like another Mons or El Alamein. Most people ski artifical snow without knowing the difference.

When Nature does do its stuff, another branch of the ski patrol swings into action: the avalanche busters. At seven in the morning they will ski above a potentially dangerous slope. 'Never below!' says Paul Miller, head of the Breckenridge, Colorado gang.

Their dynamite is set in a plastic so there is no danger of premature or accidental explosion. They ski as close to the cornice edge as they deem safe, then toss their dynamite. It usually works. A great slab of snow will crash downhill.

What if it doesn't? 'Then it's the harder way,' says Miller. He skis the top of the cornice to trigger it off. 'The trick is always to keep moving and always have a firm place to ski to.' Dangerous? 'Naw! Long as you know what you're doing.'

RUN FOR YOUR LIVES! SOMEBODY'S SPILT THE SOUP!

A GREAT LEVELLER

Skiing is probably the greatest leveller of any sport, not least because everyone dresses up for it. Or down, as the case may be. If the French *noblesse* had been capable of skiing with their peasants, their châteaux would not have been burnt down and many elegant future-generation necks would have been saved for Killy and Ellesse skiwear.

When the British aristocracy went skiing, they deserted the breeches and ties of the shooting party for their gardening clothes. Many resurfaced in the Seventies and Eighties in the nattier leisure wear of the bigger department stores. Dozens of specialist skiwear makers provide a mind-boggling assortment of

clothes for an ever-expanding market. Some people actually wear the stuff when they're skiing.

Materials may change but fashion, as ever, is cyclical. Everything comes round again in a slightly different form. Skiing has gone from dressing up to dressing down to dressing up again. The point to remember is that we all have to be the same but slightly different. Well, most of us.

The Swiss, Germans and Austrians have always dressed up in midwinter, not because of skiiing but because of Fasching, the Catholic Lenten carnival. The Swiss were at it long before Edward Whymper climbed the Matterhorn in 1884 or Sherlock Holmes fought with Moriarty at the Reichenbach Falls near Meiringen.

Turquoise, shocking pink, lime and scarlet, the okay colours of Bondi or Waikiki beaches, all become acceptable on the ski slopes to men who wear nothing but clerical grey on the 8.10 into London Bridge or the downtown services to Wall Street.

Skiing is fun. Skiing is sexy. Skiing is white, blue and grey. You can set a lot of colour into that context, as designers have found. If the US ski equipment market soared from $250 million to $1.2 billion in a decade, the ski rag trade beat that many times over. After all, you can wear an anorak or parka to the supermarket, not just the ski slopes. You can hardly say that of your ski boots.

Skiwear has made overnight tycoons of people like Paul Goldstein of Nevica, operating from a factory just north of Wormwood Scrubs and the BBC TV Centre in West London. From Japan to Norway people have gone for his colourful themes.

The bottom line, of course, is function, whatever the pretty patterns or colours. On a mountain, skiwear must repel snow, rain and cold while allowing the body to breathe through it. In the supermarket, anything with padding looks like a ski jacket. It isn't, necessarily. The Michelin man disappeared from the slopes long ago as designers discovered slimline synthetic insulates much less bulky than down plucked from shivering geese and duck.

Experiments abound. When Goldstein had a problem with linings – they weren't strong enough for a sew-in pocket – he put in a fluorescent support band and marked it with the international distress signal, SOS. A neat idea for an anorak. If you turned it inside out while lying with a broken leg on Trail Never Ever, a passer-by, or even a helicopter might stop. Along came a batch of suits, similarly marked. Ever tried turning a suit inside out, with a broken leg, lying on a ski trail? That year, a batch of inside-out SOS suits went cheap for an end-of-season sale.

'BY ALL MEANS, SIR,
TAKE IT UP WITH HEAD OFFICE'

Guide, nurse, mother, sister, consul, counsel, MC, shoulder to cry on – the travel rep is all these things and more. Just how much more, let's see. Herewith one rep's tale:

Transfer day is the hardest . . . and longest. It starts at 5 am, after three hours' sleep, with a crabby stomp through the snow to disturb equally crabby guests at breakfast and greet potentially crabby coach driver. His potential is fully realized when he sees the pile of luggage destined for the hold.

Next move – a cheery breakfast room greeting. 'G'morning . . . coach is here!' An announcement met by munching jaws, expressions of disbelief, blank stares. (Have you three heads? Have all your teeth dropped out?) Sigh deeply and stride with as much dignity and purpose as you can muster towards kitchen, grabbing cold croissant and persuading driver that he doesn't really need a second cup of coffee.

Supervise bus loading, count heads and try to stay awake at least to the bottom of the mountain. Doze fitfully until airport approaches. Grab microphone and spout gaily about marvellous week, superb bunch of folks. Inwardly shrivel at the memory of five days of rain and three broken limbs.

Deposit guests in Departure Hall and run like hell. Remind yourself never again to accept uniform with fluorescent stripe: too easily seen in densest of crowds and magnetic attraction to dissatisfied customers. Exchange horror tales with fellow reps and sup coffee until the new arrivals burst from the Luggage Hall. Seas of anxious faces: 'What's the snow like?' 'When do we get our lift passes?' Half don't know which resort they've chosen, or can't pronounce it. When questioned they reply helpfully, 'It's in France.' Or, 'It's three hours from Geneva.'

Lost luggage recovery time (half hour minimum). Lost passenger in loo time. Then off and away, microphone at the mouth. Merry prattle about the great food, the terrific après-ski, the cosy, welcoming hotel and, sotto voce, one lift open. Wary looks all round at snowless roads and fields. Don't worry, folks. Snow forecast. In the next 24 hours.

We're there! Guests are settled in rooms and informed of meal times and arrangements for equipment fitting. Know-all Neville, own Salomon bag, own skis, is the first to ask, 'Where's the ski room?' General request to park hire skis in the room allocated, also ski boots. Umpteenth person told where to get lift-pass photo. Smiling now through clenched teeth. See reflection and think . . . 'ventriloquist's dummy'.

Welcome meeting at midnight. Late arrivals always the liveliest and, usually, the most drunk. Fed and watered, they are told everything six times. Request to leave beds in rooms where they find them greeted with biggest horse laugh. Breakages will be charged to individual accounts . . . grunts and grumps. Please, not all guests will appreciate belching competitions. Second biggest laugh.

Real danger with this lot, though not uttered, that family fondue evenings will be enlivened by the latest game, condom blowing. Participants pre-stretch condoms, pull them over their heads to cover nose and mouth, then attempt to inflate them.

Following morning brings familiar scene – the Floor Follies. Everyone rolling around trying to put on ski boots. You raise your voice a trifle. 'Please everyone, it's easier if you sit on a chair.' Families are informed that lift passes require individual photos. Group pictures with four names on the back won't do. Demanding Dennis asks this time, 'If I go without breakfast will I be hungry by lunchtime?' Answer, 'Probably, Sir, but first let me take your pulse . . . what is your body-to-weight ratio?' This is somehow bitten back for, 'Skiing is quite hard work, you know.'

Wide-bottomed, scrawny, jolly, morose, reps have one thing in common – PATIENCE. A hedgehog on the M1 has better survival chances than a rep who lacks it. One other desirable quality – a philosophical nature. A holiday is not a holiday for many unless they can moan from start to finish. Deterrence need not necessarily be nuclear. It can be solved by a sentence: 'I quite agree, Sir, and by all means take it up with head office on your return.'

FROM KITZBÜHEL WITH LOVE

I first knew Austria when the Innsbruck station walls were still pockmarked by machine-gun bullets. The city rose against the Nazis before American and French troops arrived so there was no knowing who made the holes. They weren't from ski poles, that was for sure.

Among the peaks above Kitzbühel the Americans tried their first CIA tricks with a group of immigrant Germans and Austrians kitted out in Wehrmacht uniforms and sent to confuse the enemy; in so far as they knew who and where the enemy was. In fact they lost their way so many times, they ended up confusing only themselves.

Plus ça change . . . Trail maps, no doubt far superior to those of the US subversives, still leave modern-day Germans, French, Brits and Yanks anxiously grouped under the Hahnenkamm trail signs wondering where the heck they are.

Hahn, of course, means hen, and Kitzbühel (*Bühel* means hill) is just the place to chicken out from the tough old business of skiing. The little walled medieval town is Austria's queen of the travel brochures, promising and delivering lederhosen, dirndl, fig-flavoured coffee and konditorei cream cake – a well-stocked depot of all that's worth keeping in ski.

In theory it is a place of two streets, the Hinterstadt and the Vorderstadt, amid a whirligig of roads and alleyways where you can lose yourself figuratively and literally. Two pubs called the Londoner, one on each of the town's two main terraces, confuse the British as comprehensively as the Oxford Circus tube exits.

The upper one, nearer the town centre, represents the peak of skiing's après-ski Bacchanalia. A post-Hahnenkamm World Cup downhill party was got up by British proprietor Rick Gunnel and racer Konrad Bartelski. Konrad viewed Kitzbühel as his home course, partly because his father, a retired pilot, lived not far away and partly because he fell in love with his first ski instructress there. He was all of 8 years old.

No hand goes over a glass at a Londoner Hahnenkamm party, only over the top of a well-shaken champagne bottle. Racers ought really to attend in water-ski wet suits, the girls in bikinis or less. Older people are better advised to stay home with a good book.

Kitzbühel is Austria's answer to Switzerland's St Moritz or the USA's Aspen: for the skier, if you must; for those who sleep all day and gambol/gamble all night; for the halt, lame, rich or simply bogus.

All are received at a plenitude of family hotels like the old friends they are likely to become. The ancient Kitzbüheler practices of keeping tabs on your check-in slip and remembering your birthday with a card from the Tyrol in no way diminish the welcome. They seem to like you as well as your money. Kitzbühel's slopes are for the sleepless red-eyed as well as the Red Devil. Franz Klammer in high summer walked the Streif downhill course, the St Andrews of racing, and was amazed to find it a pasture from top to bottom. In other words the Alps here, formidable as they may appear, are for the most part gently gouged by Nature.

It is a benign rather than decadent place. Kitchens like those of the Erika, Tiefenbrunner or Goldener Greif hotels sit you down to meals someone has thought out and cared about. The Erika's daily programme will be underlined by a Christmas cracker motto of simple eloquence: 'A smile is the wine of life' or 'Candour is the wine of friendship'.

Guests are irresistibly drawn into 'foony' games after a top-up at the bar. Or into a minor ceremonial like the release over the Kitzbüheler Alps of a gas balloon tagged with guests' secret wishes, all of which may or may not come true. Uschi Schörer, the charming redhead who runs the place with her husband Benedict, cheated once. She glanced at one of the messages. The secret wish: 'A night with Herr Schörer'. The word got around. Ben desperately appealed the following year to a close friend: 'Please make your secret message . . . "A night with Frau Schörer".'

'There are only ten to twelve true ski countries, three of them giants, so there cannot be much money within the sport. You can play tennis anywhere in the world. You cannot ski anywhere.' Klaus Leitner, Austrian ski pool chief.

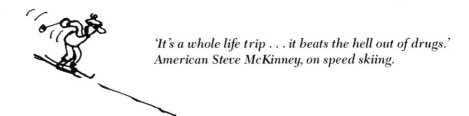

'It's a whole life trip . . . it beats the hell out of drugs.' American Steve McKinney, on speed skiing.

GETTING STARTED – SORT OF

None too high on my list of skiing achievements is my claim to have taught my wife to ski. The year was 1964, St Moritz the venue and she was apparently keen to learn. With hindsight, what she wanted to learn and what I was aiming to teach were probably two different things.

Her problems are based on the fact that she cannot get up mountains. Getting down is easier, if uncontrolled. She gets into a sweat at the sight of wheels, cogs, pulleys and, especially, T-bars. She stands for ages watching the techniques of relaxed five year-olds before venturing to offer her pass. She does so in the almost certain knowledge that hapless fellow queuers will find themselves hurtling into snow and rocks half way up, flinging themselves aside to avoid her recumbent figure. If she gets anywhere near the top, the last steep section will drain her of the last available sawdust.

Perhaps my first mistake was to bypass the simple, short tows and introduce her to the herringbone method of ascent on the nursery slopes. I then left her to herself while I went off to watch and chat with the professional racers.

The next day I taught her the plough turn and the stem christie – both just about possible in the length of piste opened up by a 50-yard climb which left her gasping and less than enthusiastic. In fairness to myself, tow technique was not high on the agenda because by and large the St Moritz of that time had no tows. Nurseries were things for nannies. What you nursed there, if anything, was a giant hangover while you waited for a stinger to get you going again around midday at the Sunny Bar of the Kulm Hotel.

In more enlightened times and *ski évolutif* – starting on short skis and gradually moving to longer – it becomes apparent that the major error was in the initial choice of hire skis. In those days, the early Sixties, you stood in the hire shop bending your fingers over the top of the skis. What you were then handed was a ski of around 1.90 metres for a 5ft 8in woman. So my plaintive partner found herself with planks which, she said, put her off before her boots were so much as in the bindings.

Then the boots themselves: not as sophisticated as they are now and very hard on the shins. How many women arrive at Geneva/Zürich/Munich airports with swollen ankles and calves which in next to no time they are trying to compress into ski boots? So, combined with the uphill slog, it meant built-in pain and Dropoutsville.

A decade later I had learned from earlier experience and taken our two children to Scotland for their first adventures. Hiring skis in a thin drizzle, not a vestige of snow in sight, might sound like McDropoutsville. Surprisingly, things worked. Aviemore was post-Modernist tatty at that point, the dry ski slope in the Colliery school of architecture, but the kids made it up and down a few times, getting the feel of things. Up above Loch Morlich, Cairn Gorm came into view like a white whale. On the ptarmigan tow at the very top, with a beginner gradient for babes in arms, I supported my wife to the top literally by carrying her. The children took some lessons from friendly Scots instructors and were off and away for life.

Not long after we found ourselves *en famille* in a John Morgan apartment in Val d'Isère. On arrival it was almost as bare of snow as Aviemore. Overnight it snowed and snowed. My ten-year-old daughter had a crisis of confidence on her first tow ride and came home black and blue. Those who can, do, those who can't, teach. My wife took time out from cooking, shopping and generally administering the 12 ft by 8 ft apartment to explain what it needed to get up a tow. My daughter listened with big solemn eyes and made it to the top the next day. Both children, now in their twenties, are inveterate black-runners. Their mother takes pride in not smothering the skiing gene.

'My grandfather quickly discovered that the British upper classes regarded it as beneath their dignity to travel under the auspices of a travel agent. It was equally not done to carry a camera or a guide book because such appurtenances "make one look like a tripper".' Peter Lunn on Henry Lunn, founder of British travel tours.

SKI PEOPLE

HANNES SCHNEIDER

Walking and running may be instinctive,
but skiing isn't. God did not invent the
parallel turn, or even the short swing. But
he invented man, and it was one such,
Hannes Schneider, from the tiny village
of Stuben, Austria, who brought the
qualities of wooden boards, gravity and
vision together to give us the modern sport
of skiing.

In 1898, Hannes prevailed upon old
Mathies, the local sledmaker, to fashion
a pair of skis for him. There was a cheese
sieve to hold his toes and a bent roofing
nail to secure the heel.

Hannes did not know how to stop, so
he opened the back door of his father's
barn and ended every run in the hay. His
skis ran very poorly, so the enterprising
boy took a lesson learned from the
labourers he watched shovelling on the
road over the Arlberg Pass, who rubbed
paraffin on their wooden shovels so the
snow would not stick.

Carl Schuler, who ran the Hotel Post over the pass in St Anton, was so
impressed by his progress that he invited Hannes to set up a ski school to help
attract winter customers. Though only a few miles apart, the burgers of St Anton
had difficulty understanding Hannes when he spoke. But a honeymoon couple
from Innsbruck signed up for lessons on 7 December 1907, and Hannes was in
business.

The Duke of Kent came for lessons and, when the future King George V
skied out of turn, he was severely reprimanded by Hannes. When King Albert of
the Belgians came to St Anton, he was put in a regular class with others of his
ability. A maharajah who peremptorily demanded private lessons was given a 13-
year-old boy as his instructor.

Far away in New Hampshire, kings weren't much in favour either. When a
certain David Gilman did George III a small colonial favour in the 'Late War'
(c. 1763) he was granted 2,000 acres in the remote, ill-endowed province.

It turned out to be a steep mountain valley about 200 miles north of the flourishing port of Boston. Gilman had something in mind nearer the coast and closer to his aspirations. He invited Benjamin Copp to build a road to his unwanted estate in the hope of selling it off. In the midst of a particularly heavy winter Benjamin packed all the family goods on a sled, harnessed the family pig, and headed north. As he noted in his diary, he 'resisted the terrors of the wilderness' for 12 years before anyone else came to settle in what would eventually become Jackson, New Hampshire.

By the 1930s Jackson was in good New England hands, and applied to Hannes to open an American branch of his ski school. It was not an auspicious Austrian début. Benno Rybizka arrived in Jackson from St Anton on 15 December 1936, and found an instructor staff of seven, the best of whom was a moderately proficient beginner. In place of the great heights of the Galzig, he had a cow pasture to work with. To complete Benno's joy, there wasn't any snow. His classes skidded round on a glaze of ice, slowed only by windfall apples protruding from the ice under the trees. Hitting them required no great technique, but it was better than hitting the barbed wire of the brook at the bottom of the trees. Benno survived, and so did most of his class.

HIC!
CIDER!

Then hard times came to Austria. The Nazis merged the German and Austrian ski teams after the 1937 Anschluss, herding the most vocal of their opponents into concentration camps. Arnold Lunn secured Schneider's release only on the promise that he would consider holding the Arlberg-Kandahar ski race in St Anton, as planned. Schneider was released and joined Benno at Jackson. Lunn considered, and decided to hold the A-K in Mürren, Switzerland. The Germans were furious but impotent.

Schneider, who never lost a downhill or slalom race as a youngster, did not write a word about his technique. He left that to his disciples. Benno served him well. His book, *The Hannes Schneider Ski Technique*, is a classic.

ERNA LOW

When a young Austrian student called Erna Low sought a way to pay her fare home to Vienna in the early 1930s, she hit on the novel idea of advertising herself in the London newspapers as a tourist guide. Five people, four men and a woman, responded to her first advertisement. So successful did it all become that Erna extended her services to summer and winter. It was the making of Britain's winter sports trade with Austria.

In the 1980s Austria could rely on more than half Britain's skiers visiting her. In precise statistical terms this meant 96 operators visiting 156 resorts carrying 350,000 skiers, with many more making their own way. As for Erna, more British have fallen on their bottoms in the Alpine snow because of her than anyone in the modern tour operator or consultancy business.

Erna might have made a lot more money if she had not been so keen to nose out new places. Her curiosity often overcame her. Hitler put an end to her travels home in the late Thirties, and she settled permanently in England. Joining the BBC at Evesham, her job was to monitor German radio broadcasts. Here she discovered other sorts of Britons from the upper middle-class; people in plus fours and ties whom, in years gone by, she would have escorted to the slopes. One of her landladies regularly took a bath when the air-raid sirens went. 'I don't want to be took when I'm not in a proper state,' she said. What Hitler's Jäger battalions would have made of her no-one will ever know!

On the buses, some of the locals would grumble to Erna, 'The worst thing about the war is all these foreigners here.' They weren't as bad, though, as some of Erna's better-educated bosses. 'The last thing they wanted to know was the date of the invasion or anything like that. It would have upset their bridge.'

Austria swiftly rebuilt its relations with Britain after the war. It had the status of a German-occupied country. Besides, the British army had rest centres in such places as Klagenfurt and Portschach, where the golf course was put back into commission as a top priority.

Soon the British, the begetters of Whymper and Mallory, not to speak of Scott of the Antarctic, were back among the Alpine peaks. The rich and famous were off to rediscover the Cresta and the Kings Bar of the Palace at St Moritz. The Austrian schilling, at 62 to the pound, exerted a no-less magic pull, and it did so for a new body of post-war Brits. The Joe Browns rather than the Whympers.

Air travel to Zürich and Munich by wartime bomber-derivatives such as the York and the Viscount was unsophisticated and none too reliable. This was the era of the Snowsport Specials, chartered by Erna Low and Major Ingham, the two major winter sports operators, to carry 400 skiers by train and boat from Victoria via Calais or Dieppe to the Arlberg. The last stop: Zell am See. A special coach was set aside for dancing half the night as they clattered through sleepy Dijon and Basle.

For about ten years all was well. One day came a disaster which changed the course of British Alpine ski history. The cold chicken they took aboard at Calais was garnished with salmonella. By Dijon passengers were queueing like mustard, for the loos. Basle was baleful, ambulances lining up. The train staggered on through Buchs and Landeck, disgorging the pale and prostrate at every stop. A day late it limped into Innsbruck. No-one ever made it to Zell am See. Some said the Austrians put a torch to the train. The days of the Snowsports Special were done.

The British have their problems with Continental Europe. If only they could spell! One man turned up at Ischgl close to the Swiss border of the Vorarlberg and wanted to know how to get to the Kaiser's palace. He was redirected to Ischl Spa on the other side of Salzburg. The first group Erna Low took to France ended up in double beds. It wasn't intentional, she thinks.

In Saas Fee, Switzerland, a male guest imprudently made advances to a beautiful young woman. She was the wife of one of the ski instructors. In the night, Erna Low was unceremoniously hauled from bed. The Englishman had been found dying in a pool of blood. Murder? They took a closer look. The sheets were red-stained, certainly, but with Walliser wine.

On another occasion a prominent judge complained his room was too noisy. He was moved to a back room. That was wrong too. It had no bathroom. Imperiously he demanded all his money back. Erna did not want to offend such an eminent figure. A court case with a judge! The weapon, though, was double-edged. At the ski school she discovered he had been using passes without paying. She instructed her solicitor to send a note saying it had come to her knowledge that he had retained money he should have refunded. If this was not returned she would sue him in open court. She trembled at her temerity. The money came by return of post.

STEIN ERIKSEN

When Stein Eriksen won the 1952 Oslo Winter Olympic Games giant slalom he was the first skier from outside the Alps to win a men's Alpine gold medal. He was handsome, stylish and glamorous, the son of a Norwegian ski-maker and he said, modestly, 'I won because I knew the course by heart.'

Eriksen then followed so many Scandinavian forbears by storming the United States. No Viking on skis could have conquered more stylishly. From Heavenly Valley, California, in 1957 he moved on to Aspen Highlands, Colorado, in 1959; Sugarbush, Vermont, in 1965; Snowmass, Colorado, in 1969; Park City, Utah, in 1973; and in the 1980s Deer Valley, Utah, the nobbiest of nob hills. Your platinum card there barely buys a day's ski ticket.

On my first ski visit to the US, Stein was master of Snowmass, the intermediate paradise with long, wide, silky trails through tree sculptures which in places could have been designed by a Hepworth or Henry Moore. Eriksen ran a lofty eye over the journalists of our motley group, two of whom were to break legs while snow-ploughing at sub-4 mph speeds, and ordered that we run a short course so he could sort us into groups. No solo flight could have been more of an ordeal. I ran my course, I thought, a touch untidily. He eyed me impassively for a few moments, as only Scandinavians can. Then: 'All right for an Englishman'.

Some time later I was researching Eriksen's special slalom silver medal at the same 1952 Olympics where he finished behind the Austrian, Othmar Schneider. I came across a rare performance. A certain Antoin Miliordis fell 18 times before, in self-disgust perhaps, crossing the line backwards. His time for one run was 26.9 seconds behind Schneider's winning time for two runs. 'All right for a Greek,' presumably.

I can also imagine Stein's words when Birger Ruud not only successfully defended his 90-metre jumping title at Garmisch-Partenkirchen in 1936, but won the downhill race too. 'All right for a Norwegian.' Norway captured 15 of a possible 18 jumping medals in the first six Winter Olympics, but from 1960 to 1984 they won nothing. Russians, East Germans, Czechs, Austrians and the old enemy, the Finns, began to carve things up on a regular basis, though Ruud, by then team manager, came out of retirement in 1948 to take the jumping silver medal.

Sooner or later the kamikaze nature of ski jumping had to get to the Japanese, and they took 1-2-3 at Sapporo in 1970. On my return home from those Olympics I stopped off for some sightseeing in Tokyo, and was joined on a tour of the city by, among others, the Norwegian jumping coach. The Imperial Palace was one of the ports of call and our guide, a charming and sophisticated Japanese lady, pointed to the palace walls. Builders would volunteer to be buried alive at various stages in a gesture to the Emperor. 'All right for a Japanese,' I could imagine Stein saying.

JEAN-CLAUDE KILLY

The lean, haunted look of the young Killy was as much a part of the Sixties image as The Beatles. His three gold medals at the Grenoble Olympics of 1968 are in the record books, but not all the mayhem that led up to them, and the furore of the races themselves and events immediately afterwards.

Killy was a derivative of Kelly on his father's side, and there was more than a touch of the Irish about the Val d'Isère teenager who caused a sensation at a ski jump in Wengen, Switzerland, by dropping his pants after take-off and finishing the jump in long-johns.

Killy suffered amoebic parasitosis while serving with the French Army in Algeria, but still qualified for the French Olympic team of 1964 in all three Alpine events. Fifth in giant slalom was about par for the devil-may-care 20 year-old.

The blue touchpaper was about to be lit. In 1966 he became world downhill champion at Portillo. In the first-ever World Cup season of 1966–67 he won 12 of 16 events, a performance not matched until Pirmin Zurbriggen of Switzerland in 1986–87. All France now waited on Grenoble. And what happened? In the major event leading up to it, the Hahnenkamm at Kitzbühel, an Austrian girl filed a paternity suit after the five-year lapse which Austrian law required. What it did not require, as many embarrassed Austrians conceded, was Killy having his laundry confiscated as surety by local police. Those long-johns again!

Killy got back his laundry and his respectability when the case against him was subsequently dismissed. But he couldn't stay out of the limelight. IOC President Avery Brundage went on the warpath against ski racers, and Killy in particular. In truth, ski, binding, boot, pole, glove, suit and, no doubt, long-john manufacturers were queueing up for his endorsements as never before. 'If a million fools buy a pair of skis because one racer wins a race on them, how can we stop them,' groaned FIS President Marc Hodler.

Then Brundage had a go. He demanded that all trade names and trademarks be removed from skis used by racers. The FIS protested that racing depended almost entirely on the goodwill of manufacturers. So they contrived one of those fudges at which ski racing excels. The racers could keep trade names on equipment, but skis would be taken from them before they could be televised or photographed at the finish.

Killy shot down from 14th place to beat his fellow Frenchman, Guy Perillat, by eight-hundredths of a second. Immediately, Michel Arpin, Killy's ski tuner, rushed out to embrace him, making sure everyone saw the word 'Dynamic', Killy's ski-maker, on his back. When the police grabbed Killy's skis, Arpin planted his own in the snow.

Killy didn't care much by now. *Paris Match*, the French colour news magazine, paid him $3,000 for a picture with the three gold models round his neck. Killy went on to become Mark McCormack's first major ski client, signing commercial contracts with Chevrolet, United Air Lines, Bristol Myers, Ladies' Home Journal, Head skis, Lange boots, Mighty Mac sport wear, Wolverine gloves, après-ski boots, etc. He became the first ski-racing dollar millionaire. And to prove the magic was still there, he became world pro champion.

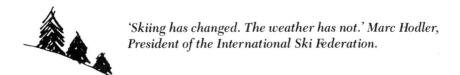

'Skiing has changed. The weather has not.' Marc Hodler, President of the International Ski Federation.

Two decades later he was still the most famous ski name in the USA. However, in Europe, his reign as President of the Albertville 1992 Winter Olympic Games organizing committee was Killy at his most spectacular – the shortest on record. The politics of his home region, the Tarantaise, defeated him where the Austrians and Swiss of the slopes could not.

A personal memory speaks volumes for his tact. In 1979 I wrote a book called *The Love of Skiing* for Octopus Books which, no doubt because of the quality of the pictures, sold several hundred thousands in English, French, Dutch and German. It included many fine colour pictures, all of which I had helped choose except one, that of the Foreword taking up one and a quarter pages.

Killy it was who wrote: 'Each year, skiing becomes more popular. Why is this happening? Skiing is not cheap and hardly a lazy and comfortable form of relaxation. But for many, two weeks' skiing is the ultimate holiday. The combination of exercise and relaxation in a vital and healthy atmosphere helps make skiing a total escape from the day-to-day jobs and chores. The concentration and physical exertion needed further helps one to forget the non-skiing world. But what compels all skiers and creates the ski-bug, is the exhilaration derived from the sport. From the beginner who has just made his first stem turn to the top racer who has put in a winning run on a slalom course, the feeling of satisfaction and achievement is intense, a moment that will long be remembered . . .'

Great stuff. The problem was that the accompanying picture was not of Killy. It was of Jean-Noel Augert, another great French ski racer, but with a mole on the left side of his face that Jean-Claude does not have. They were often mistaken for each other, especially when wearing the blue team woolly hats as here.

A month or so after publication I met Killy at a reception in Val d'Isère. He congratulated me on the book. I opened my mouth to apologize over the picture, but in a split-second closed it again. He could hardly fail to have known it was not of himself. He had said all he meant to say.

FRANZ KLAMMER
Ski-racing buffs argue endlessly over who was the skier of the Sixties, the Seventies, the Eighties . . . My nomination for the Seventies is Austria's Franz Klammer, narrowly ahead of the slalom master, Ingemar Stenmark.

From the little village of Mooswald, near Bad Kleinkirchheim, in the southern Austrian province of Carinthia, Klammer won eight of nine World Cup downhills in 1975. He set not simply a world standard for Austria, but by his

'I have never skied in Franz Klammer's shadow. I was too good for that.' Swiss downhiller Peter Müller.

'None of us should forget that Franz Klammer put ski racing on the world television screen.' Retired Canadian racer, Ken Read.

flailing, hell-for-leather style created a world television audience for ski racing. No man in world sport has borne more pressure than Klammer at the 1976 Innsbruck Winter Olympics. As 'Downhill Charlie' Kahr, Austria's great coaching maestro, once said, 'Here you can lose everything except the downhill.' Yet lose Klammer could so easily have done on Innsbruck's fiery home slope.

Bernhard Russi, Switzerland's defending champion, sped down the 3,145 metres of the Patscherkofel in 1 minute 46.06 seconds. Klammer, at the second interval, was one-fifth of a second behind yet hammered down the last 1,000 metres like a runaway train to win by a third of a second.

Television more than ten years later cannot seem to capture the noise and clatter of an 80 mph downhiller ripping into a turn and jump such as the Hausbergkante on the Streif at Kitzbühel. Here spectators and cameramen herd by the little house on the edge of the course, agog for the action as racers land in a slight compression, or knee-buckling flat section, at the same time setting up for a left turn punctuated by another jump.

But don't let's blame the poor old sound recorder. He's in the hands of his producer anyway. The racers themselves can be just as surprised by the noise they make. After a fall Canadian Steve Podborski was chatting with coach John Ritchie when Klammer tore past. Podborski could not believe his ears. 'What a racket that guy makes,' he said.

'No different to you, my friend,' said Ritchie. Podborski shook his head, scarcely able to believe it.

After his Innsbruck triumph Klammer, still half dazed, told reporters, 'I thought I was going to crash all the way.' Klammer lived on the edge, but his strength and self-confidence were such that he rarely fell. A broad-backed country boy, he took English lessons to improve his international image. When his ski manager, Gery Krims, brought over champagne to celebrate his 1977 victory at Val d'Isère, Klammer offered me a glass. 'It's not a very good bottle,' said Krims. 'Good enough for us,' said Franz with a grin.

He was all set to turn pro after winning the 1978 World Championships at Garmisch-Partenkirchen. Then everything turned sour. Sepp Walcher won the title, Klammer changed his skis, his younger brother Klaus lost the use of his legs after a downhill accident, and the great man soldiered on barely able to keep a place in the top 15. A change of boot, a change of ski, back to the traditional Austrian wood core, marriage to a sophisticated young Viennese, and four years later came victory again. And again it was at Val d'Isère. At 28 he had proved you could still win modern World Cup downhill. Next season the Klammer Express smoked to his fifth World Cup title – at 29 he had proved that old men don't forget.

At the Aspen Club the night after his final World Cup race, Klammer was alone among a thousand American fans, chomping popcorn and swilling lite beer from plastic beakers to the music of another pop veteran, Leon Russell. Next day he took off for the Las Vegas ski show and another life as an equipment and clothes entrepeneur.

Bad Kleinkirchheim now boasts a golf course as well as ski runs, and Klammer will take time off with his woods and irons in his beloved mountains. 'Still the same old Franz,' said Krims. 'He uses a driver where everyone else plays safe with a 4-iron.' 'It's why I lost ten balls last time out,' said Franz with his champagne smile.

FAST EDDIE

Fast Eddie swam – no, leapt – into my life the day I had teetered on long steps fixing a star to the top of the most ambitious Christmas tree we had ever bought. The knees wobbled as my wife passed up instructions and Sellotape strips, mostly wrong side up. At that altitude, almost unsupported, I had a weak feeling in what we still refer to, in my part of Sussex, as the lower stomach.

Eddie Edwards seemed immune to all that. Konrad Bartelski, Britain's downhiller hero of Val Gardena, now importing Atomic skis among other emeritus ski activities, had provided Fast Eddie with his wherewithal, a pair of broad, long jumping skis.

Eddie was a 22-year-old skier reared on Gloucester's nylon bristle who grew so frustrated trying to get into the British downhill team that in desperation he turned to jumping. No money, no support. In search of an 80 mph downhill fix, he hitched his way to Lake Placid, New York State, in the heart of the Adirondack wilderness. There he spotted a ten-metre high novice ski jump and within 24 hours went from ten to forty metres, taking best place in the senior category. The next size up was seventy metres, but the Americans said that was over limits. A country with a 55 mph speed restriction is also particular about 55 mph on a seventy-metre ski inrun. So Eddie took himself off to Switzerland, where few such inhibitions obtain, and shortly was jumping off the seventy-metre hill.

With his thick-lensed spectacles and bristle moustache, Eddie was happily at home in a sport of amiable eccentrics. Sondre Norheim, peasant-suited from the depths of Telemark, Norway, appeared among the gentlemen of Oslo to outski and outjump them with sensational new equipment – hand-designed, waisted skis and osier bindings which pinned his heel. Norheim scattered the opposition, returned home to a wife who begged in the streets while he whittled and whistled away, then emigrated to America and left the world his ski legacy.

Eddie, with a modest sponsorship from Cotswold Printers, Konrad's skis, some old boxing boots and a patched ski suit, set out to take on East and West Germans, Russians and Czechs with every hope in the world. The boots, sadly, did not support his landings. On St Moritz's sixty-metre hill he suffered a bad fall, landing flat on his face and breaking his jaw.

When I spoke to him he was philosophical. 'Afterwards I took the morning off, then I borrowed some French boots, 1½ sizes too big, and carried on jumping. The jaw hurt a bit, especially with the helmet on, but really I didn't feel it too much.' The French went home, taking their boots with them, and Adidas didn't have the right size. Along came the St Moritz club trainer. 'They were my size . . . 200 Swiss francs . . . beautiful boots!'

One thing worried Eddie. His glasses might steam up. 'Ninety-nine per cent of the time they clear on the in-run; when they don't I get a bit panicky. You can get turbo glasses which clear automatically – that would be very nice. I'm still very much a beginner of course, but getting better and better.'

Awed Austrians lent him their best jumping skis. Generous Germans offered a streamlined catsuit. The West German coach gave technical tips. 'My arms and head are still wrong, technically,' said Eddie. 'My takeoff is really good and so is the flight path. The German coach said I had my arms too close to my sides in flight. You need them six inches out to catch air, twisting the palms face out where you're going.' You get the image of a boy on a dolphin.

What it all added up to was a leap more confident than Icarus to 77 metres. Guy Dixon's British record of 61 metres, set at Davos in 1931, and until December 1986 the safest record in winter sport, was now as flat as week-old Guinness. 'The record was the last jump of the day,' said Eddie. 'I just kept flying and flying and landed near 80 metres. It was the best feeling I've ever had. So smooth, so good, so confident. It can depend on luck a bit. An extra gust, that sort of thing. Then you go on floating and floating. I'm a bit obsessed I suppose.' The English ski eccentric still lives.

'I'm finishing at the bottom where Ken Read finished at the top, but when we compared thoughts it was much the same. You come to Lake Louise and its bunk beds and a room smelling a bit like a lavatory. You share a room with someone ten years younger and outside skiing you haven't a lot in common. It's the sort of time you say, "Quit".'
Konrad Bartelski, British World Cup downhiller, second at Val Gardena in 1981, saying goodbye to race skiing.

THE TEAMS PREPARE

For years the first major World Cup meeting was the Criterium of the First Snow at Val d'Isère. Europe's first snowfalls year by year grew later, so areas with man-made snow nosed ahead with the slalom events, though Val d'Isère traditionally still stages the opening men's downhill event.

I stayed regularly at the same hotel as the Austrian teams. In the days when men and women all took part in the event, you would come out of your bedroom and find a row of pretty young girls, pink-faced with embarrassment or perhaps it was only exertion, in various leggy postures along the corridor. A coach would be roaring them on like an Army PTI.

The men's team spent a great deal of time playing soccer in the frozen car park. It looked a lot more dangerous than the skiing. The basement would be totally taken up by the Austrian ski armourers, waxing and filing under the harsh arc lights. They would be at it far into the night, but no matter how early you rose the hotel breakfast room would be semi-deserted. Ski racers are padding round the silent streets well before the dawn, then hurtling off to the mountain in their gaudy sponsors' cars and vans. Often, then, they would have to stand around, waiting for mists to clear or winds to abate, chatting, meditating, going through personalized loosener exercises.

No-one has an odder ritual than US Olympic champion Bill Johnson. He drops his hands like an ape, his expression becomes that of a Quasimodo. Then he shakes and shakes. I saw him at it immediately before the practice accident at Val Gardena which took him out of the 1986-87 season. I thought I had seen the portents of disaster – until someone said he did it before every run.

The slalomers find a quiet stretch of hill to practise their acrobatic gate techniques. Ingemar Stenmark often trains on another mountain, flying in only at the last minute for a major event. Media pressures are heavy on most Alpine racers, but Stenmark is alone in having a private army of pressmen.

Swedes are not necessarily Garbos, but their immense country, so thinly populated outside the major cities, gives them endless opportunity to practise silence. I remember flying into Stockholm, in what I thought was the heart of Sweden, jetting another hour north-west to Ostersund, driving another hour to Are, looking at the map, then finding I was still in middle Sweden.

I was nonetheless able to watch an English League soccer match, Liverpool against Everton, live on the hotel TV, and people spoke English as fluently as an outer British colony of the nineteenth century. Martin Bell made a great World Cup breakthrough with fifth and eighth places, then phoned his mother by radio phone from the finish area, proving we truly were part of the same world.

But the overwhelming impression was of a snow country, a place where you could listen to the silence, and not even the subsequent murder of its Prime Minister, or the Chernobyl radioactive clouds, changed things in my mind.

Stenmark is from that background. Tärnaby, his home village, is by the Norwegian border close to the Arctic circle. He claims no special physical attributes. In mid-conversation once, someone knocked over a bag. Stenmark caught it and handed it back while carrying on with his quiet observations, every word carefully chosen.

Ollie Larsson, whose laugh could bring down an avalanche, was once his ski tuner. 'He was so hard on us, so demanding. He said you ski with the inside edge of one foot or another. The five feet of inside edge had to be razor sharp.'

When my skiing gets untidy, as it often does, I still recall that advice, trying to feel the inside edge of first one leg then the other. It's one of the delightful aspects of skiing that, to a point, you share your game with the masters.

'With the Camel Jumps here (at Val Gardena), the left line is the safest, the right is the fastest and the middle is the most dangerous. The middle is where Johnson went.' Theo Nadig, on the training crash which put Bill Johnson out of the 1987 season with ruptured knee ligaments and a broken shoulder.

'It's a race for second place . . . I'm gonna win.' US downhiller Bill Johnson, before winning the downhill gold in the 1984 Sarajevo Winter Olympics.

ZIP . . . ZIP . . . ZIP ZIP

In Australia they don't beat about their bush. A winter motoring manual sold in Thredbo and Perisher, listing ways of de-icing the car door lock, advised men that they had a natural, cheap means of doing the job.

It assumed, of course, the usual intake of Fosters or Castlemaine. What it didn't provide for was the zip. Especially the sort of zip you find on ski gear. In an idle moment on a ski chair I once counted my zips. Starting from the bottom, there were two for the flares over my boots, a fly zip, two zips for my salopette side pockets, two zips for my outer anorak pockets, the main zip from waist to neck, two inside pocket zips, a collar zip for my hood, two cuff zips, a zip for my long johns, a zip for my roll top, zips for both gloves, a zip for my spectacle case, and finally a zip for my wallet. Total: 19.

In ordinary life zips can be vulnerable. In temperatures well below freezing point, operated by fumbling fingers, the quality and nature of their construction becomes critical. In my experience they are the biggest source of frustration in skiing. First, you cannot use them wearing gloves (not counting mittens). So you stuff the gloves inside your anorak. But you can't, can you, because you haven't done up the main zip. You can't, for obvious reasons, clasp your gloves under your armpits. You stuff them between your clenched thighs, bending zee knees as you will never do on the slopes.

In the bent-knee posture you close your rapidly numbing finger and thumb over the bottom right-hand corner of the zip. The hard-edged bit, the 'male' of the mechanical engineering world, you now seek to insert in the recessed 'female' bit. If you are indoors your companions will be shrieking at you to hurry. If you are outdoors the wind will score a direct hit on your midriff. Whichever way, you are likely to yank upwards with a healthy zipping noise, then find your lower midriff bared between two open flaps. In spite of all the right sounds, the zip has not zipped.

Roll on the velcro revolution. You have only your zips to lose.

FIND OUT –
AND BE FOUND OUT

No young Scoop of the ski-writing world should miss The Course Inspection. His attendance is not merely for the benefit of the Inland Revenue. It is to prove himself to himself. That he is fit to stand in the finish enclosures with the Müllers and the Zurbriggens. Indeed that he can be seen to slide the same course as they do, rather as a golf writer from time to time lends himself to the Pro-Am preceding the tournament. It is the kind of pride that readily goes with a fall.

Doing the Downhill inspection usually involves a little Press Centre detective work. It is never when they say it is, which means you have a ready-made excuse for staying in bed. After various postponements or changes you catch yourself reading the final, positive arrangement: 'Downhill start house, 8.30 am, Friday.'

You spend a fretful night listening to the wind in the eaves of your Victorian baroque hotel. Rarely are you in the Golf or the Sporting. The FIS, the Swiss or the Austrians have the corner on those ultra modern, ultra swank piles with saunas, massage parlours, hallenbads, and discreet cocktails bars with pine walls, soft green drapes and brass fitments.

Before first light you hear the crump of dynamite. For sure it has snowed steadily all night. The avalanche experts are already abroad. And soon you have to be up there among them. You twist and turn, conscience and sense of duty struggling with sloth. Curiosity wins, as it so often does.

At Crans-Montana for the World Championship downhill inspection you made your way up via the Grand Signal *télécabine*. Although it was barely light, downhillers, coaches and servicemen of 34 countries ghosted past blank-eyed apartments and sleeping hotels towards Grand Signal.

Grand Signal was like a sealed-off Victoria or Grand Central station at commuter hour. As I groped my way into a six-seater *télécabine*, a downhiller jumped in after me – Peter Wirnsberger, Austria's World Cup champion. We chatted amiably enough about this and that. At the halfway station, the ominous sounding Cry d'Err, the doors opened and out he bounced. 'It's too dangerous for me today. Best of luck . . .' And with a light laugh he made for the restaurant. The weather is in fact too bad for racing practice. But heavy snow and fog are not stopping the press inspection.

Circumstances now trap you. Only 19 of the thousand-odd media people in Crans have turned up. At least four of them are ex-racers turned commentators. One is Karl Schranz, an all-time great. We take the cabin car to the very top, Bella-Lui at 2600 metres, and wait in the start house while squads of soldiers try to trample all the new snow. In the driving snow they look as puny as starlings. Boubi, who designed the course, is our guide. We can hardly desert him now. We push Schranz to the front and one by one, Swiss, Austrian, German and English, take off. Boubi shouts 'Langsam . . . lentement' or 'Slow'. Unnecessary, really. The start chute is 40 degrees, but the last thing you are doing is trying to go fast.

The sideslipping soldiers, working in echelon, have left scraped patches in crude diagonals. You try to turn on these and spear the heaps they have left with straight skis. Otherwise your feet are your eyes. You and the racer may be on the same course, but they are different worlds. He is trying to go as fast as he can. You, for the most part, are doing quite the reverse. He has 225 centimetre skis for the job. You have 195. Even on inspections, you remind yourself, racers can fall over. Once we are halfway down we begin to see more readily. Tractors have got to work and the snow is beautifully groomed. You begin to enjoy yourself – hugely. Boubi stops to point out course features. You look back at the Mur de Vermala and he tells you it is 61 degrees. You scarcely believe you came down it.

Worse, far worse, was the Hahnenkamm inspection at Kitzbühel. The Streif is like the White Cliffs of Dover piled one on top of the other. The first cliff after the start – ferocious in itself but flattened out of all perspective by the TV cameras – is the Mausfalle. One year I slithered to the edge and waited a full five minutes before plucking up the courage to sideslip the near vertical face. The outside of the course was unskiable bare rock. The course was the only way down. A group of Austrians ducked through the fence to join us. Just below me, an Austrian girl hooked a ski tip in the wooden palings bordering the course and fell. It was like seeing a mountaineering rope break with 25 people on it. One by one they took each other, like the proverbial pack of cards. Skis tweaked off as bindings snapped. Twenty-five people landed in a heap 100 metres below. No-one was hurt, but not for the first time you wondered at the courage of people who skied the Mausfalle at speeds up to 80 mph.

'I saw the fence and went into survival mode.' US
downhiller Mike Brown, after a near-crash at Val d'Isère.

'Downhill racing is the classic flight or fight syndrome.
The only thing I want to do when I am going fast is to go
faster. You don't think. There is no thought process in ski
racing. You react like an animal.' Canadian World Cup
downhill champion Steve Podborski.

FRAGMENTS USA

The wide open spaces of the American West breed easy-going attitudes in the lift lines. 'Have a nice day, sir,' from the lift attendant isn't a ladle of consumer maple syrup. It's an invitation for some easy chit-chat, possibly with a student of philosophy or the classics.

In France you often feel that *maman* is actively encouraging her *enfant* to pin you by the tails of your skis while their family surges in front. In the lift lines of Colorado, Wyoming or Utah you automatically alternate, one by one or two by two. Queuing is a gentle social occasion, an opportunity to ask where people are from and how they are enjoying themselves. The cry 'Single' will speed you along the line, maybe to join a builder from Baltimore, perhaps a long-haired, copper-skinned beauty, mysterious as Cleopatra behind her mirror glasses. In neither case will you encounter snooty indifference. Soon you will know the rock-bottom price of four-bedroom houses in downtown Baltimore, or the 'in' bars and restaurants of Aspen's *fin-de-siècle* Mall.

You sleep in the Rockies higher than you ski in Europe. Resorts like Aspen (7,900 ft) and Vail (8,200 ft) are higher than the take-off point on most Austrian runs. Because their latitude, in European terms, is that of Sicily, the tree-line is much higher.

America is explicit. Runs are carefully classified. Each area will point out that its standards are its own. Demarcations between green, blue and black signposted runs, the usual colour index in ascending beginner, intermediate and advanced order, are peculiar to that resort. Million-dollar insurance settlements (the exception rather than the rule) make ski area managements a touch nervous but ever more consumer-conscious.

Nerviness doesn't extend to clients. Americans ski in stetsons, bermuda shorts and bikinis when the weather gives them half a break. Base lodges may look like hangars for noisy old Constellations. The Happy Hour booms with amplified country and western, rock and roll, shouted greetings and parched throats slaked with lite beer and popcorn.

SUN VALLEY KNOW-HOW

Sun Valley in the State of Idaho is known for many things. It was the first purpose-built US ski resort. It attracted movie celebrities like Gary Cooper, Jimmy Stewart, Clark Gable, Norma Shearer, Claudette Colbert, Ingrid Bergman, Jane Russell and writer Ernest Hemingway.

It put together an American, Averell Harriman, polo-playing chairman of Union Pacific Railroad, who wanted places for streamlined trains to go, with an Austrian aristocrat, Count Felix Schaffgotsch, who had a developer's eye for good ski terrain.

It found grown men who, since boyhood, only wanted to run trains, and who went on to invent chair lifts. In skiing terms it was like inventing the wheel. Mechanically, all that skiing had so far to get any distance up mountains was a rope tow, T-bar or cabin car.

A man named Jim Curran had once loaded bananas from hooks. Humans or bananas. What was the difference? So the chair lift was born, except they built it too low to the ground, estimating four feet of snow when it more often turned out to be six.

Sun Valley in those early days had skiers bending their knees heavenwards. Railwise crews used their expertise to dig skier cuttings, but the learning process was tough. Holding a balancing rope in one hand, your poles in the other, and waiting for the chair to hit – that, too, was tough.

Drop-outs and drop-offs come in all shapes. Eventually Sun Valley discovered the Lady Who Would Not Get Off. Nearing the top of the first lift, she was seen to tighten her grip on the safety bar. As she passed the 'Open Safety Bar' sign, she wrapped her arm round the chair vertical. 'Get off, get off!' yelled the attendant as the chair swung round towards the bull wheel. 'No, no,' said the frantic lady, 'I'm going all the way to the top!' She didn't quite make it. Centrifugal force took over and she was out of the chair like a slingshot. Everything can – and did – happen in Sun Valley. She survived.

FOUR DOUBLE FAULTS
American hospitality and American competitiveness are equally renowned. One of my earliest experiences of the first quality led to one of the most memorable examples of the second.

The World Cup downhill at Aspen is a good enough peg for a week of jollies. The Aspen Winternational has an enormous round of social occasions – La Grande Affaire, a tuxedo-and-glitter charity dinner; celebrity races; firework displays that illumine 14,000 ft mountains, and so on.

At a reception at the Snowmass Club, which has nautilus apparatus to make a nuclear submarine look old-hat, Stu Campbell, technical editor of *Ski* magazine, invited me down to Heavenly Valley, on the California-Nevada border. 'Share my place,' he said. Stu, like many Americans, wears a variety of hats. He is technical director of Heavenly Valley ski area, one of the biggest in America. He has written best-selling books on the vegetable and the underground house. He'd heard I was doubling up as a boxing reporter, covering a title fight between Colin Jones and Milt McCrory at Reno. And Heavenly was 60 miles down the road, through part of the legendary Donner Pass, gateway of the Sierra Nevadas, then down the east fringe of Lake Tahoe to Heavenly in the corner.

I could ski in the morning, and pick up fight stuff in the afternoon ready to file early next morning (we were seven hours back). An irresistible idea. The next season I was back for the World Cup ski finals. Stu at once introduced me to Dick Needham, editor of *Ski* magazine. 'Got some ladies to ski with us,' Dick carols. 'Sure you won't mind.' So I met Eleanor Killebrew and her almost identical sister Jeannie.

'Remember the Toni twins?' said Dick. Of course I did. 'Then try and tell which from which.'

Thirty years ago their likenesses were on hoardings throughout North

America and Britain as home perm kits became the rage. Originally, professional models were used in the promotion. Then someone had the notion of running a contest for identical twins. Jeanne and Eleanor Fulstone were 19-year-olds from Smith Valley, Nevada, gutsy daughters of a rancher. Someone put in their names and the agency offered them a five-year contract.

Hundreds of proposals followed their appearance in the ads, but when they married it was to two men they had met skiing. Jeanne wed Fred Corfee, and when Eleanor's first marriage ended in a divorce she married Hugh Killebrew. Hugh's great dream was to rival Alec Cushing, who gained the 1960 Winter Olympic Games for Squaw Valley, at the north-east corner of the lake. Tragically, Killebrew was killed in 1977 when his light plane crashed, leaving Eleanor chairman of the board and two young sons, William and Michael, to help her cope. Heavenly's 12,000 acres of exquisitely groomed slopes to the north-west overlook Tahoe's glittery blue expanse, and to the west the dun of the Nevada desert.

A pleasant day's skiing, so warm you could tie your anorak round your waist, was followed by a party at Ellie's place where everyone who was anyone in World Cup skiing could dance the night away – or that was the way people were made to feel.

Next came Vancouver and the 1986 International Ski Federation congress. Ellie was there. So was I. In the huge hotel complex, committees dwelt earnestly over ski slope safety regulations, World Cup scoring rules, critical points for the jumping hills, professional and amateur issues, and, bare knuckles showing, whether the new skating step should be banned. (The Russians, most conservative of all, said yes.)

In the central halls, a gastronomic war raged among those seeking world championships or Winter Olympics. On the notice board were the diversions, and one of them was for a FIS doubles tennis tournament. Ellie had entered her name. Under 'partner' she had scrawled, 'I'll find someone.' It was irresistible. 'What about me, Ellie?' I scrawled, adding my name. Next day: 'Great! See you Thursday, 2 pm.'

Ellie looked very smart and suntanned. I remembered she had a court or two in her garden, I think a harbour as well. She nodded at our opponents. My heart sank. Two women, two American women. One was in charge of US Masters' skiing. That means a lot in the USA. The other was the wife of an airline pilot representing the US Ski Federation in some capacity. Both were entirely charming but also, clearly, had courts in the back garden.

'Two women,' said Ellie. 'John, we can't be beaten by two women!'

I am fairly athletic but do not have a court in my back garden. The local public courts see me about six times a year, mostly in the four weeks after Wimbledon. My service is strong but erratic. It was a good game as far as it went. My turn came to serve and save the match. Crunch followed crunch, as jet-propelled serves hit the wire and fell back into our court. Four double faults. We advanced to congratulate our opponents. They had never conceded a point without a fight. Ellie shook my hand, and gave me a thin smile. When I get to Heavenly again it will only be in an old Ford car.

'Ronald Duncan's performance was severely hampered by bruised shins and excrutiating pain following the removal of a toe nail. Despite the considerable handicap, Ronald completed the course.' British Ski Federation Hand-out, 1987.

CHAIR RIFT

It's a little known sporting fact that Japan was chosen at Garmisch-Partenkirchen in 1936 to host the Fifth Winter Olympic Games at Sapporo, on the most northerly island of Hokkaido, in 1940. Because of the Sino-Japanese war and World War II it was 1972 before the Land of the Rising Sun caught up.

Japan at this point had never so much as held a World Cup ski race, but their reputation was for efficiency. At ski jury meetings conducted in English, which the Japanese seemed to understand well enough, heads would be nodded and promises made. Much to the surprise of FIS officials, lapses were many and often.

BANZAAAAAAAAAEEEEEEEE

Suddenly someone got the message. The Japanese understanding was less than pride would permit. A switch to German meant an interpreter was brought in, and from that moment all was sweetness and light on the slopes.

All, that is, except for one thing on the giant slalom course. The chair lift was, by European standards, very small. Not only that, it had no foot rests. Quickly the racers discovered that the tiny seats without rests were giving them cramps. David Zwilling, of the Austrian team, was in one of the lead chairs and found a neat solution – he turned around in the chair and rode up backwards. The virtue was obvious to all the others following, and when the attendant at the top of the lift looked down the hill all he could see was backs. Clearly these could not be experienced skiers if they did not know how to ride a lift. Fearing catastrophe, the operator threw the switch.

Of course racers like nothing less than a stalled lift. Underneath, though, was three feet of new snow. Zwilling jumped off followed by every other racer on the line. It was an hour and a half before the FIS could get the Japanese to start the lift again.

There was another problem. The organizers were doing a prodigal job clearing off all the new snow with squads of soldiers. The idea was to get down to the fine, hard surface prepared for the race. To help with that, an aluminium chute, four feet wide, ran the length of the hill, and scores of soldiers were shovelling the new snow into it. A great plume of powder snow was flying out of the bottom, certifying all the effort.

Irresistible forces now came to bear. The racers made a few powder runs in the wonderful new snow, but kept eyeing that chute. Finally Erik Haaker, a powerfully framed Norwegian, could bear it no longer. He skied over to the chute, and before one of the shovelling soldiers could know what was happening he found himself pitched into the chute. Down he went, faster than Haaker could ski it, before hurtling into the huge snow bank being created.

For a moment there was stunned silence. Could this lead to a new Pearl Harbor? First there was one giggle. Then another. Suddenly the whole regiment broke ranks and, one after the other, threw a shovel full of snow into the chute and jumped on top of it. Order was restored, but not for a very long time. One commanding officer was no doubt mightily grateful that between 1940 and 1972 things had changed. It didn't mean throwing himself down the chute on to a waiting sword.

SNOW QUEEN MEETS SNOW PRINCESS

Erna Low did not blush when a young woman journalist described her as the Snow Queen. She giggled. As doyenne of the snow tour operators, she had been in the business for well over 50 years and was not easily surprised or put out. She knew who she was.

As happens, however, to all good veterans of the slopes, a day comes when it is time to stop. Skiing, that is. Erna's own last day is firmly etched in her mind. The circumstances, mind you, were not exactly ordinary. She had been informed, in the special circumlocution of those times, that the girl with the famous mother would be in the Benenden School party.

She was in no doubt who they meant. The problem was that, as with the rest of the party, The Princess Anne would have to share a room with three others. A further problem was that the allotted room had three good beds and one camp bed. Next . . . goodness! The daughter of the famous mother was going to arrive late. All three decent beds would be snaffled by the three who got there first.

By the time the advance detective arrived to scout things out, everything had been arranged. Somehow a fourth decent bed had been crammed in. The three other girls dutifully turned their faces to the wall when appropriate. Good behaviour was maintained for the duration – but they were anxious moments for those in charge.

Erna, still a touch distracted, hung herself around with her usual camera gear and set off for the slopes. She knew the press were not supposed to be around. She also knew that no pictures were allowed in the papers. But some photographic record was permissible, she felt. The equipment was heavy, and made skiing difficult. Suddenly she caught an edge and slipped into a river.

OOH LOOK! PRINCESS ANNE!

HELP!

'I thought I was going to drown. "Hilfe! Hilfe!" I shouted.
Some Germans were passing and they came over to help. But as
one tried to pull me out, he fell in too. It was a terrible mess,
and terribly dangerous. Luckily the others managed to
get both of us out. But that was it. No more skiing.'

APRÈS-SKI – THE REAL THING

I am grateful to an old friend, Jimmy Riddell, for putting après-ski into universal perspective in some lines he penned for the Kandahar Club's 60th-birthday magazine. It was on the subject of Torvill and Dean, and the pleasure they gave in winning the ice dancing gold medal at Sarajevo.

'I can well remember,' he wrote, 'when I was first taken to Mürren in 1920 – four years before even the Kandahar came into being – that people went out to the Alps for 'the Winter Sports' rather than for any specific activity to do with snow or ice. It was quite common then for our visitors to inquire of one another, 'Are you a skater or a skier?' and there were – I seem to remember – rather more of the former than the latter.'

There were two great ice rinks at Mürren, the Palace and the Kurhaus, where people would stand and watch those lucky enough to be able to waltz together. Jimmy goes on, 'There were carnivals and fancy dress evenings by torchlight, and real live musicians played from covered terraces. Vast tablecloths of well-prepared ice were viewed by people sunning themselves in deckchairs.

'Particularly do I remember . . . the mercurial and dazzling skater Diana Kingsmill (later Gordon-Lennox) who, with her monocle and forerunner of the mini-skirt, performed miracles of movement at about Mach 2. When I was 16 or 17 she tried to teach me to waltz. She was the first girl I ever tried to kiss – late at night on the ice rink it was. Sadly, neither of us succeeded in our projects.'

Some girl, Diana. She finished 32nd in the 1936 Olympic downhill, and last but one in the slalom, racing with her arm in a sling and wearing her monocle.

In the Alps these days the risks, challenges, speed, changing terrain underfoot and scenery have removed skating as a ready alternative. No longer, either, at the finish of the ski day do people stomp around in ski boots to live trios. You could somehow achieve it with fox-trots and waltzes, never with rock and roll and its derivatives. The tea dance is virtually dead.

In Austria, family hotels have borrowed to their limits building hallenbads and saunas. The exercise bike stands at the pool side. The ladies don't wear monocles in the saunas. They don't wear anything at all. The jacuzzis bubble and hubble in the US condos. Couples and families down Coke and lite beer and plan evenings at the Mexican restaurant. Then, for the younger ones, on to Dirty Dick's, the King's Club, the Number One, the Ambassador. All talk, no listen. Gels dancing together. It's the same the whole world over.

'So many thought us eccentrics, freaks, kamikaze people.
Driving a London cab is more dangerous.' Britain's
Graham Wilkie, after beating the world speed ski record
over a measured 100 metres with 212.5 kph (132.05 mph).

'Skiers here are afraid of nothing. I have seen them ski
down slopes which elsewhere would have been recognized
as a meadow, but no – here it is considered an excellent
skiing slope, just as long as there's a little snow buried
between the grass and the heather.' Early post-war visitor
to Scotland.

THE WORST SKIER IN THE CABLE CAR

Once, travelling on the Chanterella funicular railway at St Moritz, John Hennessy, then sports editor and ski racing correspondent of *The Times*, looked lugubriously around at young men dressed like skiing Uhlans, at trims girls, their eyes concealed mysteriously behind dark glasses, and murmured, 'Do you ever get the feeling that you must be the worst skier in the whole of the cabin?'

The answer, of course, was yes. A third of the people were only on the train with the intention of developing a tan, as soon became apparent. Skiers have a constant battle with the ego. Not too much. Not too little. Tony Jacklin once said about golf that if you stand and stare long enough at a single tree it will quickly become a forest.

Some mental blocking out is necessary. Some is not. Getting to know yourself is a help. It's no good pretending in the funicular or cable car that the movement and height are not worrying you when they are. It is a natural reaction, shared by many, which will be further compounded when you slide on your skis, particularly in the beginner stages. The first movement on skis, the first loss of familiar orientation as the hill begins to slide past at increasing speed, is a moment of terror for most adults. Children, being closer to the ground, and in any case more flexibily muscled and boned, may not mind so much.

It's all to do with the eyes and middle ear and physical, rather than mental, reactions. You find the same symptoms in other situations. Most people have felt a slight sickness when travelling in a train with their back to the engine and seeing things flash past in the other direction. The sensation is vertigo. Much the same is happening on a cable car several hundred feet off the ground, especially broken ground which imposes further focal strains on the eyes. They won't exactly be standing out like organ stops, but simply to know that the eye is in a process of adjustment often eases the sensation of dizziness or sickness. It's a good thing to focus on something constant, on the person you are with, on the ceiling, or, if the worst comes to the worst, a really good-looking young lady. Provided, of course, that you don't attract even worse trouble from the boy friend.

Never underestimate the effects of altitude. Alpe d'Huez is a somewhat sybaritic resort in the French Alps east of Grenoble. It is high, like most third-generation French resorts, with an outdoor swimming pool looking invitingly blue under the noon sun. Even in February the Savoie resorts of the South-west Alps are touched with a Mediterranean sense of snow beach.

Outdoor swimming amid banks of snow is, after all, exotic and even on the initial plunge the water felt agreeably warm. The pool was about 35 metres long and, a reasonably strong swimmer, I struck out briskly with a crawl. At 20 metres the crawl had dissolved into a panicky dog paddle. Five more metres and I was sinking. I had failed utterly to allow for altitude.

Air will be thin here, less oxygenated. The heart has to work harder to achieve a simple objective like bending down and fixing ski-boot clips. Fatigue will come much sooner than you would expect from the activity in hand. Skiing is a risk sport, but the risks which are less easily calculated, or not calculated at all, are the most dangerous. Like the man unaware that he has drunk too much, the tired skier loses objective judgment about his own condition and becomes a danger to himself and others.

Look at it another way. Floating in the Alpe d'Huez pool with eyes closed, I could still point accurately to my left foot, or know whether my right leg was bent, without any sighting aids. This is because of – wait for it – my vestibular apparatus. This, in fact, is situated on each side of the head next to the ear and is made up of two simple but clever organs. The first is a jelly-like structure called a utricle, containing many fine nerve hairs. If the head is bent to one side the weight of the jelly makes the hair fall to that side, passing the information to the brain. If a skier leans to one side to absorb a bump, the message is relayed and the brain at once leans the body the other way to maintain balance.

The second organ consists of three small circular tubes, linked rather like a clover leaf, but at right-angles to each other, and filled with fluid. They lie on each of the planes of movement, the fluid inside adopting a position according to the place of the head in a given plane. The three together exactly define the position of the head. These organs send their messages flashing to the brain, which, with its 1,000,000,000 nerve cells, programmes a physical response. The worst skier in the cable car is a cleverer scientific vehicle than an Apollo spacecraft. So that's one more reason to relax, and let Nature do its work.

'TV aims are not our aims. We must be fair to competitors at all times. TV is a perfect medium for swimming, because conditions are the same for everyone. In our case snow conditions can change dramatically. One reason why we embrace artificial snow is because it increases the possibility of the best skier having the best chance.'
Marc Hodler, president of the FIS.

LONGSHOTS IN SARAJEVO

There's nothing like a Winter Olympics to discover the oddball. At Sarajevo one altogether too-serious young journalist argued fervently to anyone who would listen that the Winter Games were about two things – the men's downhill and the figure skating.

Sarajevo was cram-full of gossip writers and ego blowers trying to find things to write about other than the endlessly colourful events. When all else failed they would stick a clumsy moon boot in Gavrilo Princip's reverently preserved concrete footprints and manufacture a war-to-end-all-wars story. If Archduke Francis Ferdinand's corporal chauffeur had not taken a wrong turning . . .

Comes the moment, though, when both gossip and specialist writers get the story they love. Olympic courses are nearly always easier than World Cup tracks like the Streif at Kitzbühel or the Lauberhorn at Wengen. Sarajevo, with its artifically built-in bumps, was hated by the specialists because any one of the top 30, as opposed to the top 15, might win it.

The Austrians, victors in every World Championship or Olympic downhill from 1974, with their usual intensity had a race within a race in the three practice days, finally eliminating Harti Weirather. So, out went the world champion while skiers from the Lebanon, Morocco, Senegal, Bolivia, Mexico, Korea and Egypt entered the start gates.

Calm was not the exact word for Jamil El Reedy of Egypt. At 18 he had been sent into the desert by his father. He was to live alone for mental purification. 'I was alone in a cave for a month coping with boredom and loneliness,' he said. 'There were scorpions and spiders to live with. But that was not all. As an alternative

TRY AGAIN — BUT
THIS TIME REMEMBER....
USE THE INSIDE EDGE!

discipline my father had me wash out the walls of a room with a toothbrush and mug of water.' A university place at Plattsburgh, New York State, and some racing experience on Whiteface mountain, the somewhat downmarket site of the 1980 Winter Olympic downhill, followed. The start gate at Sarajevo represented only a kindly Kismet.

Elsewhere in Sarajevo a youngster barely able to parallel ski wandered into a local shop to acquire a somewhat bulky, out-of-fashion anorak, and 175 cm skis. His name was Ahmed Ait Moulay and he was to race the Olympic downhill for Morocco. Yugoslavia, as anyone who did not know quickly learned, is a country of divided tribes, religions and races, but almost uniform generosity.

Vinko Bogatej, director of Elan, the Yugoslav ski maker for Ingemar Stenmark and Bojan Krizaj, promptly provided a pair of downhill skis for Moulay. El Reedy too. 'What is a pair of skis to us?' he asked rhetorically.

Elan began with a young Slovene partisan, Rudi Finzgar, carving solid ash skis to help survive against the well-equipped Nazi mountain troops. When the war ended he set up shop in a disused textile shop at Begunje and formed the Workers' Ski Co-operative. Ten employees had grown to 1,100 and Elan ranked with Fischer, Blizzard and Atomic behind the French giant, Rossignol, at the time of Sarajevo.

But would the people of Sarajevo, city of 450,000 in the strongly Muslim province of Bosnia-Herzegovina, take to skiing? Three years later, on the warm and sugary snow of Cairn Gorm mountain, in the heart of Scotland's central highlands, Rok Petrovic, the greatest ever Yugoslav racer, was doubtful. The 1986 World Cup slalom champion drew a line on the snow.

'All Yugoslavia's best skiers, men and women, come from an area only 50 kilometres apart,' he explained. 'They are Slovenians, from the north. In Sarajevo they are team people, they love soccer. For skiing you must be an individualist, and the individualists are from Slovenia.' Encouragement for every longshot.

'In ski you win in the mind . . . you lose there too.' Ermano Noggler, Ingemar Stenmark's trainer.

'The loss of a life is . . . well . . . the loss of a life, and that's something you can't take away.' Secretary, British Winter Olympic team.

'There are three ski resorts in Lebanon. One is occupied
by the Syrians, another by the Israelis, and in the last one
you are advised to ski off-piste because you might stray
into some minefield.' Martin Chilver-Stainer, British ski
industry expert.

DRIVING PLACES

The courtesy on Japanese roads is the highest I have ever encountered. The Sapporo Winter Olympics of 1972 gave me some of the reasons.

A day or so before the Games I showed my British driving licence to the hire-car people to be told I should have brought an international licence. My national licence could be validated if I presented myself to a driving centre for 'certain inquiries'. The Press Centre provided an attractive young woman interpreter-driver and off we set.

Long terraces of shops and single-storey apartments pressed hard on streets disappearing into infinity, but at last we pulled up behind a low shed with a corrugated roof. Behind it, as far as the eye could see, was a forest of traffic lights and signs, pedestrian crossings, and every hazard known to motorized man. No Japanese is allowed on the roads before proving that he can master this maze.

I was bidden to follow my raven-haired guide through the shed door. First, I took off my shoes. I was rewarded with her most soulful smile. Inside, six men squatted on the floor round a central stove with a chimney disappearing up through the ceiling. In a corner a colour television – not general in those days – was showing a ski-jump documentary. For the six men, I was the day's emergency. I smiled, and was given six ear-to-ears in return. In Japan, a smiled greeting is *de rigueur*. Anything else is a sign of hostility. There was no chair in the place. They pulled up a low table and gestured that I sit on it. I smiled appreciatively but squatted on the floor. My prolapsed lower veterbrae groaned, but not out loud. Their smiles, if anything, grew wider. The opening courtesies were done with.

The problem now was the licence. My interpreter went into a lengthy huddle with one of the six before returning with a request, expressed as an apology, that I accompany her to a neighbouring room. Her complexion held the perfection of a Japanese blossom tree, a gentle pink, now a touch pinker, against the purest white.

In the next room a woman in traditional kimono sat over a contraption like a Victorian child's game. It fulfilled the same function as a typewriter, entering appropriate personal details in the blank places of a form by the depression of an indexed lid. With more than 50 Japanese characters to choose from it proved a lengthy process. The micro-chip revolution was getting into its swing but it had not yet reached outer Sapporo; not, anyway, when it came to form filling.

The process eventually done, I was passed through another door to be confronted by the periscope of a nuclear submarine. 'Prease, rook thlough here,' I was bidden. I gripped the bars, turned my cap back to front, and squinted at the enemy. A set of verticals and horizontals converged and separated. I was asked to follow a pinpoint light. Could I see this? Could I see that? I could.

Everyone smiled. I was safe to drive a Toyota on a Sapporo road.

CHAINS

One of my earliest shock-horror memories is of a dungeon in Hastings Castle on the south coast of England. There they had a hollowed stone, head high, which showed how men were kept in chains for decades at a time.

Any sign in any language demanding chains on my car fills me with something of that dread. As we set off for Sapporo that day, my navigator and I, we did not dream of the trials ahead. My navigator was journalist colleague Chris Brasher, steeplechase gold medallist at the 1956 Melbourne Olympics. Nor did I know that we shared the chain dread in common – until, as we drove up to the ski course, a Japanese policeman suddenly confronted us.

It was pretty obvious why he was waving us down. Men miserably lying under cars in a layby were not sacrificing themselves for the Emperor. They were fixing their chains.

'Don't stop, don't shop,' Brasher screamed at me, the driver of the little Toyota. 'Press, press,' he yelled at the little policeman who was about to throw himself across our Toyota's bonnet. In truth we were late for the race, a giant slalom. I swerved and kept going, expecting any moment some massive retribution. Fortunately the road was just about driveable. We did make it for the start. But I still have a conscience for the little man.

No doubt, had I used chains on another occasion, I would not have gracefully left the snaky, icy road to the little village of Jertzens, in the west Tyrol, one day in 1985. I was on my way to the British championships. It was late afternoon, the sky clear, the road suddenly like glass. I was fractionally out of the ruts. The front wheels of the Golf simply failed to answer to the steering wheel going round a corner. There was a precipice to the off-side. I had just enough control to guide it broadside to the nearside snowbank where it came gently to rest. A set of burly Austrians, stopping at once, quickly pushed me out.

Over the next few days the snow kept falling, the temperatures fluctuating just under and over zero, the worst possible conditions. Soft ruts, icy ruts, hard pack, soft pack. Chains, the manual says, should never be driven above 25 mph, or more than 10 miles without changing the chain position on the tyre; and never at all on bitumen or dry gravel.

If you have to fit the chains yourself, you can try driving on to them. First you carefully lay them out like a snake skin. When I tried to drive on to them in the Golf they simply curled up round the wheel, boa constrictor fashion. Why? I had gone to the trouble of finding a flat lay-by, having already noted the manual's sage words about never trying to do it on a hill. Or you can opt for the jack-up method. My trouble was, I had omitted to bring a 10 cm^2 board or waterproof ground sheet, as advised, on my flight into Innsbruck, before I hired the car. This is essential. In the semi-darkness, I confess, I also had trouble finding the jack, let alone trying to operate it. The third recommended method – two spare wheels ready-fitted with chains – was never a starter. Not with a hire car.

So, like millions before me, I decided to let a garage do the job. Problem. The chains were wrapped around the front wheels, hopelessly entangled. I set off, heart in mouth, and at once hit an Autobahn junction. No way was I safe on that. But how many service stations were now open on an Austrian side road? Slowly I made my way back up the mountain, remembering a garage ten kilometres back.

The attendant listened to my halting German. He shrugged, stuck a pneumatic jack under the front axle, and undid the tangle in less than a minute.

BEDSIDE SKIING

A SPIN IN THE MOUNTAINS

Sage yachtsmen will tell you the first lesson about boats is that they have no brakes. A savvy mountain driver will remind you that you may have brakes, but if you stamp on them hard on an icy road you might just as well be in a boat.

I have once turned a car round, and once gone off the road. The first was a hire car out of New York, its suspension wrecked by the rock-and-roll roads of the near-bankrupt city of 1980. We made it to Lake Placid, a town of four roads and one set of traffic lights, staging the Winter Olympics in the heart of the Adirondack wilderness. On the way, a State trooper waved me down in nowhere land, around 100 miles short of my destination. Somehow my wreck had made it to 68 mph according to his radar. Maybe it was the British accent, maybe his Olympian spirit, but he let me go with a warning.

US policeman were even more wonderful a few days later. En route for the Olympic Village from my quarters in Saranac Lake, the dear old Ford Fairlane started to jib on a hill not yet cleared of its snow. My throttle thrust was a touch too sharp and the automatic engaged second gear with my front wheels not quite straight. The powered rear started to swing. It is a bad, bad moment. Whether you do the right thing, steering into the skid as the manuals tell you, is a matter of instinct. If the rear of the car is skidding to the left, you turn the front wheels to the left and vice versa. Of course, the good old Irish way to get out of a skid is never to get into one. I took both feet off everything. With nothing coming the other way and the car going very slowly, I let it swing right round. Being a spectator at your own funeral cannot be much different. It kept right on going, never checking, before sinking side-on into a snow bank.

I gave the throttle a gentle jab and drew a chainsaw noise and no discernible movement. I started to engage first gear and reverse in a rocking motion. No result. Suddenly a stetson hat filled my side window. 'You're gonna need some help, fella,' a voice boomed.

Your sense of helplessness is equalled only by your foolishness. 'Get into neutral and I'll try and make it easy,' he said. He had a four-wheel-drive Chevvy with a pair of king-size mattresses attached front and rear. I have been kicked out of bed, but never by a bed. Slowly he eased me out like a peanut from its shell.

I was his twelfth emergency of the morning and it wasn't yet eight o'clock. Americans, I discovered, even those living in the immense State of New York, extending right up to Buffalo on the Great Lakes, were not necessarily much better with their winter warms than the silly old Brits.

People from places like Albany, the State capital 100 miles away, lived with central heating and air-conditioned cars. Many had no idea of the severity of mountain region weather. Some really did walk miles from a parking lot to a slalom or downhill course in soft shoes, or sneakers. This in an area which, at the previous year's pre-Olympic cross-country skiing, suffered temperatures of minus 34° Centigrade.

JACKSON HOLE

Distance in the USA lends not only enchantment but sometimes a sense of unreality. I once took a lift, with a Canadian photographer friend, from Aspen, in the heart of Colorado, to Jackson Hole, Wyoming, the mountain State immediately to the north.

We left early evening but the road to Glenwood Springs was still buzzing with Happy Hour dawdlers returning to Denver. At Glenwood Springs, unlike the rest, we turned left, not right. After that, in ten hours' driving, we saw only five more travelling cars and a belching rogue truck determined to leave us for dead.

Cutting across the north-east corner of Utah at a little town called Vernal, we stopped off for gas and refreshment. 'Where you headed, Mister?' a small boy with big round eyes asked from the next table. It was late. He and his family were the only other diners. Jackson Hole, I told him. Which way was I going? 'That road's closed,' said the lad. 'We've a four-wheel drive and we only made it behind a plough. There's sure some storm out there.'

I gave the news to Chris, my Canadian friend, after he came from the rest room. 'These goddam Americans can't make cars and they sure can't drive 'em in snow,' he snarled. He claimed to have personally taken apart and put together every component of his 10-year-old Volkswagen estate. I got him to ring the American AA. There was a major storm. The major Inter-State highway we'd intended to take was closed. The storm was whizzing around, tornado fashion, striking indiscriminately with great dumps of snow.

Chris very reluctantly took out his maps. There was another route to Green River, across a desolate high mountain plateau. Chris was determined to make it. We filled our spare petrol cans. Gas stations are anything from 150 to 200 miles apart hereabouts. Oh, yes. The engine had been missing slightly. He fiddled around with the injection system wires and said it was better. We were in survival mode, it seemed.

The streets of Vernal were deserted as we left. We had seen its lights, like a distant forest fire, from fully 50 miles away. Now, eerily, its comforts receded in our mirrors. Signs at different points told us we were at 10,000 feet. I listened to the engine note and watched for signs of the phantom storm. Here and there writhing snow banks closed on us, but always there was enough of a gap. You remembered

the cruel statistics of American storm casualties, and understood why. Help would probably be a long way away. My ears began telling me we were descending. More lights far ahead. Green River. A staging post.

All activity was frozen in the early-morning light. A single gas station served us by cold fluorescent light. Money first, fuel after, US fashion. We got to bed in Jackson Hole around 5 am. Chris was on the road again by 9 am, Calgary bound. Just another 15 hours or so.

An hour later Harry Baxter, Jackson's marketing manager, was showing me round what was to take my vote as the greatest little ski resort in the world: three hotels and a few condominiums off the Snake River Valley, at the feet of the Tetons, mysterious as Indian totems. Off their flanks were so many miles of queueless runs they could give you a certificate for the vertical you skied. Yellowstone Park was not far off but a sense of isolation permeated the place. Harry's children had only eaten meat from moose he'd killed, skinned and hung from canoe expeditions up the Snake.

Going up the day's last tram – US for cable car – Harry asked me how many Brits might find their way to Jackson. The State capital was 500 miles away and not much else between. Perhaps a few adventurers from home, maybe, following in the footsteps of the Earl of Murchlie, who impressed even Jim Bridger and Kit Carson with his dead-eye marksmanship and hunting skill. Maybe a few businessmen, up from Salt Lake City, San Francisco or LA.

With that a ski stick fell across my toe. 'Sorry,' said a distinctly English voice with a West Country burr. He was a post-graduate from Bristol doing temp work in Los Angeles. 'Mind you don't step on him,' he said of another young man squatting just behind us. 'He's from High Wycombe and he bites.' Three of the 16 people in the day's last tram were Brits.

'Just because it's their country they always think they should go first.' British skier in French Alpine lift queue.

'The French are not normally a Nordic skiing nation.'
Ron Pickering.

HOW WOULD YOU LIKE YOUR INJURY?

Skiing sometimes is not so much a sporting activity as a damage limitation exercise. The kind of damage differs from generation to generation. In the Thirties *the* sound of the slopes was not the yodel but the dry crackle-pop of fracturing femurs and tibias.

If we give over the Forties to the chatter of Stens and Schmeissers, the Fifties went on where the Thirties left off. Wood skis, Kandahar bindings and converted climbing boots kept us well and truly plastered, the noise level that of a stroll over dead twigs on a little-used country path.

The Sixties introduced metal and fibreglass skis, and more sophisticated step-in bindings. Leather boots were better designed for skiing, climbing high up the calf, and for another style of injury. Together with the sharp report of the breaking shin came the seductive thwuck of parting achilles tendons.

Thermoplastic, polyurethane and adiprene booted us into the not-so-brave knee world of the Seventies. Ankle and shin injuries all but disappeared. At last, with these stiffer man-made boots holding the ankle firm, the part of the body taking most of the stress was the one least capable of bearing it, the good old knee. The era of the crushed cruciate, the loosened ligament, the carved cartilage, the mushed meniscus, was upon us. With it came a low, sinister noise – the graunch!

The skier pinging out of his bindings might occasionally find relief in an old-style shoulder fracture. Usually, though, it was the knee surgeon who was sent for, and in the Eighties he continues to come. It is not usually a fatal injury, just deeply incommoding. The arthroscopic surgeon with his little mirror and light needs an incision of only three-eighths of an inch to peer around and peel off a bit of offending cartilage. This way, if you are lucky, you can be in and out of his clinic or hospital in a day or two.

The Swiss downhiller Pirmin Zurbriggen won at Kitzbühel with a damaged knee cartilage, and inside three weeks was World Champion at Bormio, thanks to the arthroscope. The Canadian Todd Brooker had a knee that from nine operations looked like a mangle-wurzel. He wasn't really sure it was nine operations, he'd just lost count.

Knee injuries taught the Austrian-born Marc Girardelli and Canadians Steve Podborski, Ken Read, Dave Irwin and Todd Brooker, outstanding winners all, more about themselves than they really wanted to know. All suffered not simply cartilage injuries but ligaments severed, torn away at the bone root, or shredded like pieces of old rope. Rehabilitation was long and arduous.

Let's assume, for a quiet life, that you have damaged one of the two crescent-shaped knee cartilages, the meniscuses, and one of the four ligaments keeping the knee in place. An arthroscope enters one side of the knee and a surgical knife the

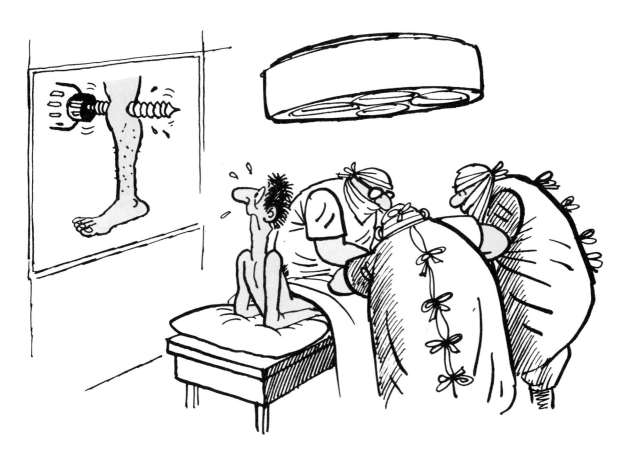

other. In a specialist US sports medicine hospital a TV screen monitors the action on the operation room wall from a camera inside the arthroscope.

A meniscus on the screen looks rather like a clam. It is something of a bathoscopic world, for the clam of an injured meniscus looks as if it has been nipped by a crab. The surgeon shaves at the meniscus so pieces flake off and are sucked out of the joint. Once the tear has gone the surgeon removes his arthroscope and goes to work on the ligament. The knee he now slices like the Christmas capon. If the ligament has pulled out of the bone it may need a spot of power drill. A puff of smoke, a smell of burning, and, presto! it is grafted back in. Polyester, Goretex, twisted thigh gristle, they're up to all sorts of substitutes if the ligament truly has broken like a hank of old rope.

The knee has to be restored only so that you can bend it again. 'Bend zee knees' is not merely a stale ski school cliché. It is a genuflection to the skiing gods.

NOW HEAR THIS

'You must pay you rent in advance.
You must not let you room go back one day.
Women is not allow in you room.
If you wet or burn you bed you going out.
You are not allow to gambel in you room.
You are not allow to give you bed to you freand.
If you freeand stay overnight you must see the manager.
You must leave you room at 12 am so the women can clean you room.
Only on Sunday you can sleep all day.
You are not allow in the seating room or in the dinering room when you are drunk.
You are not allow to drink on the front porch.
You must use a shirt when you come to the seating room.
If you cant keep this rules please dont take the room.'

Notice in the historic Christiana Inn, Whistler, British Columbia.
You knew where you stood in those days. The Christiana didn't.
They knocked it down for redevelopment.